A DARING ADVENTURE
STALKED IN THE CATACOMBS

Peter Reese Doyle

PUBLISHING

Colorado Springs, Colorado

STALKED IN THE CATACOMBS

Copyright © 1993 by Peter Reese Doyle

Library of Congress Cataloging-in-Publication Data
Doyle, Peter Reese, 1930-
    Stalked in the Catacombs / Peter Reese Doyle.
    p. cm— (Daring Adventure Series)
    Summary: Mark and Penny Daring and their friend David Curtis
are in Paris for a holiday and act as couriers for sensitive information. When they are attacked on a tour of the catacombs under
the city, they become separated and must find their way back
alone.
    ISBN 1-56179-142-3
    [1. Paris—fiction.] I. Title. II Series: Doyle, Peter Reese,
1930- Daring Adventure Series.

Published by Focus on the Family Publishing, Colorado Springs,
Colorado, 80995

Distributed by Word Books, Dallas, Texas

Edited by Etta Wilson
Cover illustration by Ken Spengler
Cover design by James A. Lebbad

Printed in the United States of America

94 95 96 97 98/ 10 9 8 7 6 5 4

For

Jonathan Jackson Doyle

Whose integrity, chivalry, and breadth of interest form the model for the honorable young men portrayed in these books.

CONTENTS

CHAPTER 1

PARIS

"**W**e're almost four hundred feet above the ground!" Mark exclaimed, awed by the spectacle. All of Paris was below them!

Mark, his sister Penny, and their friend David were at the second observation platform of the immense Eiffel Tower which soared almost a thousand feet into the air. Visible for miles around, the giant iron structure served as a watchtower for vast areas of the great French city. The sky was clear, but the wind at this height threatened to blow them off the huge tower. Of course the guardrails prevented that, but the force was frightening.

"Man, I'd love to sail off this tower in a hang glider!" David said, his brown eyes alive with excitement. Taller than Mark by two inches, David was lean, broad-shouldered, and very fit. Both boys wore dark trousers and long-sleeved shirts. Now they wished they'd worn jackets!

The three of them had just arrived at the platform and were wandering around the open spot with other tourists. The great French city was a magnet, drawing multitudes of people from every part of the world,

1

month after month, year after year. And thousands of them came to the Eiffel Tower to see the vast panoramic view of the great city.

"The wind's ruining my hair!" Penny said, clutching her hands vainly to her head.

"You mean, it's *rearranging* your hair, don't you?" Mark teased. "Why do girls always talk about their hair being *ruined*, when they just mean *rearranged?*" He shook his head as though puzzled and grinned.

"Oh, you know what I mean," she laughed. Then she pointed to the far reaches of the blue horizon. "Look at the size of this city!"

"And look at the river right under us," Mark exclaimed, gazing down at the Seine. "Wonder if we could dive in from here?"

"You wouldn't even come close!" David replied. "You'd decorate the street below—*if* you cleared the bottom of the tower."

"You might hit those pigeons," Penny warned. "Look at them! So far below us!" She pointed to a flock of the lovely birds soaring a hundred feet below them. The sunlight flashed from their wings as they sailed gracefully around the great structure.

"It's not often we get to look *down* on flying birds!" Mark commented. Fascinated, he squinted in the bright sunlight as the birds flew out toward the horizon.

"Feel it move! This whole huge tower is *moving!*" Penny said suddenly. "Does the wind make it do that?"

"It sure does," Mark answered, "but I doubt if that's

what you felt. The thing only moves a few inches in the strongest breeze! You just felt the wind."

"But I thought it was too heavy to move—millions of pounds of iron!"

"It is," Mark replied. "Fifteen million pounds, in fact, if I remember correctly."

"'Remember correctly'! Who are you kidding? You just read that in the guide book," she retorted.

"I also know how many rivets are holding all these pieces of metal together," Mark added smugly.

"I'll bite," David said. "How many?"

Penny, her dark brown eyes sparkling, laughed at the way the wind blew David's hair to the left side of his head.

"Oh, I'd say something in the neighborhood of two and a half million," Mark answered speculatively.

"What a genius!" his sister observed, shaking her head. "You probably know how many metal pieces there are in the whole tower."

"Twelve thousand," Mark replied promptly. "Give or take a few."

The three wandered around the eastern side of the platform. "There's the Louvre!" David pointed to the giant museum. "I can't wait to get in there!" The huge building that housed the world-renowned museum towered over surrounding structures.

"We'll have lots of time for that," Mark said. "Dad wants us to work with Keno, and Keno's been loaned an office in the Egyptian wing. We'll be right in the middle of all that. It's the biggest palace in the world! There's a million things to see inside."

At seventeen, Mark was David's age, and a year older than his sister. Heavier than David, he was solidly built, with a broad open face and perpetually friendly expression.

Penny shivered in the wind, and Mark put his arm around her. In spite of wearing a heavy white sweater, she was nevertheless chilled by the strong cool breeze.

"Want to go back down?" Mark asked.

"Not yet," she replied. "There's too much to see. Let's look at the guidebook and spot some of the sights. Mom and Dad said they'd join us when they were through in the shop."

Mr. and Mrs. Daring were in a shop below, looking for souvenirs for Mark and Penny's younger sister and brother. The young children had remained with friends in Africa while their parents visited Paris on business.

Mark, Penny, and David strolled around the platform, checking the map in the guidebook, gradually getting a feel for the fabulous city. They tried to spot the office building where their Dad was going to spend the next week.

"It's west of here, not far from the river, and right in the Latin Quarter. We should be able to see it," she said.

"And to think that we were in Cairo day before yesterday!" David exclaimed. "That was a shorter visit than we'd planned."

"It was also a lot more exciting than we'd expected!"

Penny added. Her eyes grew thoughtful with the memories from the previous week, as the wind continued to blow her light-brown hair around her slender face. She was four inches shorter than her brother's five feet, eleven inches, slender, with a very quick wit and—David thought—a beautiful smile!

"Well, there were some dangers all right!" Mark agreed. "But let's concentrate on our vacation in Paris. We never thought we'd be here! Look! Is that the Cathedral of Notre Dame?" He pointed toward the east where a huge structure with flying buttresses towered above a small island in the river.

"I think so," David answered. "At least, that's where the map says it should be." He looked at it for a moment. "Gosh! It's huge! And the island it's on does look like a ship—just like the guidebook says."

"When will we go there?" Penny asked.

"Let's ask Mom and Dad," Mark replied. "They're going to take us to all the major sights—and the restaurants," he added.

"The restaurants!" David added. "Which reminds me, isn't it time to eat? Penny's got to be hungry!"

"But we just had breakfast!" Penny protested. "How can you two be hungry now?"

"You're right, of course," he replied. "It was just a thought."

"David, you're as bad as Mark about eating," she laughed. "Do you want to end up being that fat?" She poked her brother's flat, hard stomach.

"How about a little snack?" her father asked behind her. The three turned and saw Mr. and Mrs. Daring, gift packages in hand.

"Well, if you insist, Dad," Mark answered doubtfully. "Actually, I was going to wait a couple of hours—until Penny got hungry, that is. But if you insist—" He headed for the elevator.

"Wait just a minute, young man!" his mother objected. "I just got here. I want to see the view before we watch you gorge yourself again." A tall, friendly woman, she teased her children as much as her husband did. She had dark hair, greying at the temples, and wore a plaid scarf to keep it from being scattered by the wind.

She walked to the eastern rail, "Oh, Jim, look! The Cathedral of Notre Dame! and the Opera!"

Ecstatic, she pointed out sight after sight to her husband. She knew Paris well, having lived there for a year before her marriage. But she and her husband had not visited it recently. David watched her face glow with pleasure as she pointed out the famous places. Clearly, she loved this city. She loved the French language also, which is why her children had learned it so thoroughly.

After a while, Mr. Daring asked his wife, "Ready now, Carolyn?"

"All right," she said, "but we've got to come back here again."

"Agreed," he said. The five of them went to the

door and descended the huge tower.

They spent the rest of the day visiting majoi tions, shopping, and eating marvelous food. Ma.. and David were awed by the military items they saw in the museums: uniforms, models of fortifications, heavy guns, mortars, and weapons ancient and modern.

And Penny and her mother spent the whole afternoon visiting clothing stores. After all, they were in Paris, fashion center of the world.

The cab let them out that evening near a bridge that spanned the river Seine. "The name of this old bridge, believe it or not, is 'New Bridge'!" Mr. Daring told them. "And it was new—in 1607! It was the first bridge to be paved and to have houses built along it, but the houses are gone now. Let's cross over. I want to take you to a rather famous little restaurant."

They sat on the outdoor terrace of the tiny La Rose de France and ordered supper. The breeze from the river penetrated the spaces between the buildings around them. People were speaking in a dozen different languages, and wearing costumes and clothes of every variety. The youngsters had never seen such sights.

"This is fabulous!" Penny exclaimed, her eyes shining. "No wonder you've loved this city, Mom. There's something new every minute!" She watched an Asian family pass by, the mother carrying a little baby, the father and older children aiming their cameras in every direction. A crowd of Germans followed and then a group of people who appeared to be Turks.

"Are the waiters the only people who speak French?" Mark asked. "I thought we'd get to practice. All I hear is Japanese, English, German, and who knows what else!"

His mother laughed. "You'll hear plenty of French, Mark. Just be patient."

"I want to tell you something about Paris," Mr. Daring said. "The city began right here on this island—and on the other one there." He pointed toward the Isle St. Louis to the east. "This is where the present Paris originated. A tribe called the Parisii settled here in the third century before Christ. But Caesar's legions captured the place in 52 b.c., and from then on it was a Roman fort and colony. For five hundred years, in fact.

"Paris has had a remarkable history," Mr. Daring continued. "There are several hundred thousand university and graduate students in its various colleges and universities. They come from every nation in the world. Twenty nations speak French as their national language, and twenty-two more speak it as a second tongue. No city in the world influences so many other nations and their leaders."

He thought about that for a minute. "It's tragic that there is so little gospel witness here."

"But there're a lot of churches, Dad," Penny observed.

"You're right, Penny. And millions of people say they belong to the church. But few of them actually go to church. It seems to be more of a cultural tradition rather than a living religion."

"Maybe the Lord will let us talk with someone about Him," Mark said.

CHAPTER 2

THE LOUVRE

Awestruck, Mark, Penny, and David followed Mr. Daring to the sixty-foot-high glass pyramid that rose from the courtyard of the Louvre. Light from the sun's rays flashed off its many triangular panes, making it look like a giant diamond. Daring had a special pass which let them avoid the lines of tourists and visitors waiting to get tickets. Once inside the glass pyramid that housed the new entrance to the historic site, they took the escalator down.

"Look at the light through the glass panels," Penny marveled, craning her neck to see the novel construction above them.

"This is the famous pyramid of the American architect, I.M. Pei," Mr. Daring said. "When President Mitterand awarded him the contract to design a new entrance, the French people were outraged that someone from outside their country got the job. But they were even more outraged at what he did. A glass pyramid—in front of these old buildings! It was quite a controversy. Pei said a pyramid reminded people of the fabulous Egyptian things inside the museum."

"I think it looks weird," Mark concluded.

"But it's so *interesting!*" Penny observed. "And look at all the light it lets into this underground cave." Her photographer's eyes were fascinated by the play of light coming through the remarkable glass structure above them.

"Let's find Keno. He's expecting us," Mr. Daring said as they reached the lower level. He took the kids by interior escalators to the vast Egyptian section on the second floor. "The Egyptian Gallery is below us," he explained, as they walked down a huge hall, "but a lot of things are on this floor as well. And Keno's been loaned an office here."

Striding vigorously, they finally arrived at a small office where they found Keno. The tall Egyptian rose from his desk, his solemn face breaking into a gracious smile as he shook hands with them. They'd last seen him at the airport in Cairo just two days before when he'd come with Paul Froede to see them on the plane to Paris.

"Well," he said, his affection for the three teenagers showing in his dark eyes, "I see your dangerous adventure in my country hasn't harmed you!"

"But, Keno," Penny replied, "we never did get to talk with you about your escape! Uncle Paul told us about your race across the desert, but we never heard about the rest of your adventure."

"Oh, I just took a fast drive across the sand, hoping to find a village with a radio or phone so I could get the police to come rescue you three." He beamed at them. "I think Paul's call reached the police first, however."

Then he turned to his desk and pointed to the papers and drawings on which he'd been working when they entered.

"But look at these! The director here has let us have drawings and pictures of the tablets we've come to decipher. I've studied some of them already and they're fantastic!"

Mr. Daring and the youngsters crowded over his desk as he pointed to a large diagram. "That's the tomb we were in just a few days ago," he said. "That's the part we were exploring. Now, look here."

He brought out more papers. These had photos of hieroglyphics on the left-hand side with wide spaces between each section. On the right side of the pages, in spaces left blank for the purpose, Keno had made his translations.

"Along with my translations, I've made comments to help us in our excavations. I'm cross-referencing these paragraphs, which I've numbered, so we can coordinate what we learn as we go along. The museum director lets me photograph the tablets—which are kept in a locked room, Jim—and then I translate them here." The tall Egyptian's face glowed with excitement.

"How's the security, Keno?" Mr. Daring asked. He asked the question in a casual manner, but something in the way he spoke let the kids know that he was quite serious.

"Excellent, Jim, excellent! I couldn't ask for more."

"What kind of security, Dad?" Mark inquired.

"Well, we had some trouble getting cooperation from the Louvre," his father answered. "Remember, the Museum of Egyptian Antiquities in Cairo has the tablet made by the original architect of the tomb you three were trapped in last week. That's how Keno was able to learn so much about it before he actually got inside. But centuries ago, it seems, a part of that stone was broken off and brought to Paris with a lot of other priceless loot foreigners were taking from Egypt. That broken part had specific directions to the treasure room and to other parts of the tomb as well. Our people here were trying to get at those directions to save us time as we began our explorations."

He looked sharply toward the door. He listened for a moment, glancing quickly at Keno. David, the closest to the door, thought he heard footsteps moving quietly away.

After a tense moment, Daring continued. "As it turns out, there was a spy on the staff here at the Louvre. He was blocking our search for information because he was working for Hoffmann's people. The police found him out finally, but not before he'd given Hoffmann's gang the directions to the tomb's treasure room."

He looked somberly at the youngsters. "We need you three to carry Keno's translations of the tablet from here to my office and keep the flow going. No one will suspect you. And you'll have plenty of time for sightseeing."

"This information really helps us, Jim," Keno said. "It will save us much time as we open up the rest of the tomb. And it's also an inventory of the contents of each room. What a find! No wonder Hoffmann's people were so anxious to steal that loot. The treasures are worth millions of dollars, either on the open markets of the world or in the black markets."

His eyes grew thoughtful. "But they belong to my people, the Egyptians, and to their history. And I'm so thankful that Hoffmann's gang of thieves did not get them! Thanks to you three and to Paul Froede," he added, looking gratefully at Mark, Penny, and David.

Daring nodded and smiled. "We'll let you get back to work, Keno," he said. "Don't forget, we're expecting you to join us at the restaurant for dinner. Tomorrow the kids can start bringing your work to the office where my staff will put it into final shape before sending it to Paul Froede in Cairo."

After saying good-bye to Keno, they left the office and went down the long hall, past priceless relics from the ancient world. When they finally came to the shop in the glass pyramid, Jim Daring bought them a map of the museum.

They stopped at a restaurant inside the Louvre, ordered drinks, and learned from Daring how to find Keno's office on the map of the giant building.

"You're sure you've got it?" he asked. "Penny,

you've been watching the people instead of the map!"

"Oh, Dad, the boys will get me there," she laughed. "Besides, I can't take my eyes off the wonderful costumes here! These people are from all over the world!"

"Is that all you want us to do for you here, Dad?" Mark asked. "Visit Keno and take his work to the office?"

"That's all," his father replied. "And see the sights of the city! We wanted to give you a little vacation after your experience in Egypt. Your mother and I won't take all your time," he promised, smiling. "I've got work to do with the French branch of the company our mining firm is working for. Your mom has friends to see. So you three will have some time to yourselves each day."

Then he looked at Penny. "Just don't let this young lady out of your sight." He squeezed his daughter's hand affectionately. "She's too pretty to be let loose in *this* city!"

"Aw, Dad," Mark teased with a perfectly straight face. "David will watch her enough for both of us! Why don't I just go with you to your business meetings?"

David's face got red. Penny's did too. Mark winced suddenly as she kicked his leg sharply under the table.

Mr. Daring laughed. "Leave David alone! I want *both* you boys to keep an eye on her. I promised your mother that you would."

He looked at his wristwatch. "We'd better go. Your mom asked me to pick up some postcards."

They left the restaurant and went to the shop nearby.

"This place sells five million postcards a year!" Daring told the three. "Look at the variety!" The place was packed with people crowded around the stands of post-cards and pictures. Here they browsed for a while, each selecting several cards. Then they paid for the cards and left the shop.

A powerfully built man in black turtleneck and dark trousers had been leaning casually against the wall out-side the shop, looking as if he had nothing to do but smoke the cigarette that dangled loosely from his thin lips. A long white scar ran from his left ear to his chin, strikingly white against the dark tan of his face. He didn't appear to notice when the four left the shop, but when the escalator had carried them halfway to the ground floor, he straightened, shouldered his way through the crowds, and followed.

Neither Daring nor the kids looked back as the escalator took them up to the glass pyramid which opened to the street. Even had they done so, how could they have picked out one stranger from the mobs of people who packed the museum?

CHAPTER 3

THE GIRL FROM ANOTHER WORLD

Mark, Penny, and David sat around a small white table in an outside cafe at the Place St. Michel, absorbed in watching the people on the street. They'd found this cafe the day before, and now, in the middle of the morning, they were enjoying pastries and the crowd.

"Let me read about the history of this place!" David said with guidebook in one hand, chocolate pastry in the other. Penny noticed a smudge of chocolate on his chin.

"Give us a break!" Mark pleaded. "You've done nothing but read history since we got to this city." He rolled his eyes at Penny in pretended anguish.

"What a Philistine you are, Mark!" she scolded. "Don't you want to do anything but eat and drink and gawk at the tourists? Here we are in the center of Western Civilization, and David's trying to educate us. For shame!"

She wore a pretty white dress and white shoes. She

looked, David thought, like a classical goddess from ancient mythology, transported through time to twentieth-century Paris.

"I've already told you how many rivets there are in the Eiffel Tower, Penny!" Mark replied. "How much culture do you want?"

"Rivets! Isn't that just like a Philistine? Rivets! It takes more than rivets to make a civilization." She tossed her head, and her light brown hair swirled around her face. "Don't mind him, David," she said in a pitying tone. "He can't help it."

"I think you're right," David agreed with a smile. "Now about the Place St. Michel where we're sitting: it reeks with history! It's right on the River Seine," he said, pointing to the river and speaking in a professorial tone. "And it's one of the gateways to the Latin Quarter."

"They call it the Latin Quarter," Mark interrupted, "because for hundreds of years that's the only language you could speak in this part of the city. It's the language they spoke in all the schools of Europe—nothing else was allowed. That way, students from all the nations of Europe could come here to study and talk to each other."

"How did you know *that?*" Penny asked in genuine surprise.

"Oh, I just pick up these cultural facts as I go through life," he said. He leaned back in his chair casually, the picture of pretended boredom.

"He's right, Penny," David confirmed. "That's why it's called the Latin Quarter. For seven centuries it was an independent city within Paris—a city within a city—where the people's allegiance was bound to the Pope in Rome. The laws of Paris had no jurisdiction here. It was a tremendous center of learning. Scholars came from all over Europe to study under world-famous teachers."

"What did I tell you?" Mark asked. "I guess I know all about culture and stuff like that, Sis! In fact," he added, "the students learned early that if they robbed a shop or wine cellar in Paris they could escape into the Latin Quarter. The city police had no jurisdiction here!"

The three of them turned suddenly at the sound of raised voices from a couple at the next table. Both were wearing worn dirty jeans and dark shirts, and they had long uncombed hair. They appeared to be having an argument. The girl in particular looked very unhappy with her long blond hair falling around her pale sad face.

"Want to move, Penny?" Mark asked, noticing his sister's grave expression as she looked at the couple.

"No, Mark, but doesn't she look unhappy?" she observed quietly.

"She'd be pretty if she didn't let herself look so scruffy," Mark said, in an equally quiet tone.

"They sound like Americans," Penny said.

"Lots of kids in our country look like that," David observed. "Mom says they don't seem to respect themselves as people did when she was growing up, and they don't care how messy they look. It's sad." He looked at Penny with sudden seriousness. "Please don't ever change, Penny."

Startled, she looked in his eyes. He was very solemn. Time seemed to stand still as the two looked at each other. "I won't change," she said.

In years to come, David would remember this moment many times.

Suddenly the young man at the next table jumped up. Red-faced, he slammed his hand on the table and stalked off in a rage. Tears ran down the blond girl's face.

"Why don't you boys go take pictures or something so I can talk to her?" Penny asked.

"That's a good idea," Mark replied.

He and David rose and walked down the street. Mark's dad had told them not to let Penny out of their sight, so they wandered around the perimeter of the outdoor cafe, looking at the surrounding buildings, pretending to be oblivious of Penny. Mark took out his compact camera and began to take pictures.

Penny regarded the crying girl for a few moments. Then she got up and went to the girl's table. She spoke quietly, not wanting to attract the attention of the many tourists around them. "Can I help?"

Startled, the crying girl looked up at her. "No," she answered angrily. She took out a cigarette and lit it.

Penny waited a couple of minutes; then tried again.

"You're American, aren't you? We are too. Do you mind if I sit down?"

The girl looked coldly at Penny for a long moment. Then she thawed a bit and nodded. "Is that blond guy your boyfriend?" she asked as Penny sat beside her.

"Mark? No!" Penny replied, laughing and utterly surprised. "That's my brother! What made you think he was my boyfriend?"

"He held the chair for you when you sat down," the girl said. She wiped her eyes with her sleeve.

"He always does that—when David doesn't beat him to it!" Penny replied. "Their dads raised them to show respect to girls. Frankly, I like it."

"Seems silly to me," the girl replied. "I can move my own chair."

"So can I," Penny agreed with a smile. "But it sure is nice. I like it!"

The girl was obviously stunned. "I never heard of a brother doing that! Mine don't. I don't know *any* boys that hold chairs for girls. I wouldn't know what to do if they did."

She smoked a moment, and Penny wondered what to say. In some ways, the girl seemed to live in another world, and Penny didn't want to offend her by a careless remark.

The girl spoke first. "That other boy likes you. I can tell."

Penny blushed. "Oh, David's a good friend. We've known him a long time."

"I guess you sleep with him, then," the girl said casually.

"Of course not!" Penny was shocked. No one had ever said anything like that to her.

It was the girl's turn to be surprised. "What do you mean?"

Penny's face was red—and angry. "I mean just that!"

"You don't mean you're a virgin!" She started to laugh, then realized that Penny was very serious.

"Yes, I am, and those boys are too!"

An awkward silence hung between them; neither knew what to say, and Penny was still angry. Then she calmed down, struck again by the girl's genuine sadness. She knew anger wasn't going to help at all. She decided she might as well introduce herself.

"My name's Penny."

"Mine's Sandra."

Slowly, tentatively, the two girls from different worlds began to talk.

CHAPTER 4

BEAUTY AND THE BEAST

Focusing his camera on Penny as she talked with the girl, Mark had already taken several pictures. David asked to borrow it, walked a few feet away, and focused on Penny from a different angle.

Looking through the viewfinder to frame his picture, he was surprised to see a stocky man in black pants and turtleneck shirt walk around a group of people, stop suddenly to stare at Penny, then back up several steps, and position himself behind a lamppost.

David looked up quickly from the camera. The man was obviously shocked to see Penny and hadn't noticed David and Mark across the cafe. David switched on the telephoto lens, focused on the man who was half-hidden behind the lamppost, and waited.

"Mark! Back out of sight for a minute. Hurry!"

Mark obeyed without question, stepping behind an umbrella that covered the table beside him. He turned and looked away from where David was focusing.

"What's up?" he asked tensely.

"A guy just saw Penny and backed away in a hurry as if he didn't want her to see him. Then he hid behind a lamppost. He's leaning on it now, smoking a cigarette, trying to look casual. But I know I saw him jump when he saw her. Wait a minute—he's looking around the post now!"

David snapped a shot and then another. "Got him! But he moved. It might be blurred."

He turned to Mark. "That guy is looking at Penny again. She's still talking to the girl so she can't see him behind her. Look around. Is anyone watching us?"

Both boys turned casually and surveyed the scene. David held the camera before him as if looking for another picture to take. Mark played the typical tourist, apparently just gawking at buildings, but his eyes swept the crowds, searching for anything suspicious. Neither boy noticed anyone watching them.

"That's strange," David said, troubled. "Why would that stranger not want Penny to see him? And why would he hide behind a lamppost so he could watch her?" A chill had come over him. Memories of their recent dangers in Egypt crowded into his mind. Then he had an idea.

"What do you say we test him out? I'll go get Penny and take her across the street to another spot. Then I'll pretend to take her picture. You stay here and see if he follows." His face was stern. "If he makes a move at her, I'll lay him low," he said quietly.

"So will I," Mark said.

David looked at the great open square between the buildings and the river. "I'll take her to the bridge. See if you can get a good picture of him when he follows. I'll use Penny's camera and take some pictures with her zoom lens. Maybe I can get a good shot of his face. Then you can follow and join us across the bridge if he gets too close."

"You bet!" Mark replied. He didn't like the idea ·of anyone shadowing Penny either.

David handed Mark's camera back, then headed through the tables for Penny, making a point not to look in the direction of the man who was still watching her. He worked his way through the tables filled with people drinking coffee and eating their morning pastries until he came up behind the girl to whom Penny was talking.

"Hi!" he said.

When Penny look up, he frowned a warning over the girl's head; then smiled when the girl turned around and looked at him.

"This is Sandra, David," Penny said. "She's American too, and we've just gotten to know each other."

"Hi," David said, smiling at the girl. Then he looked back at Penny. "Excuse the interruption, Penny, but I've got an idea. Let me take your picture over by that bridge. I've been looking around, and that's the best place to get a picture your mom will like."

Penny had seen his warning frown, and she knew

her mom hadn't asked for a picture. Something was up!

"O.K.," she agreed, picking up her purse and camera case. "Can we talk later, Sandra?" she asked earnestly. "I want to hear more about Chicago."

"Sure," Sandra said, listlessly, "if you want to. I mean, I'd like to—if you would."

"I would," Penny replied. She looked at her watch. "What about three this afternoon. Can you come back?"

"Sure," Sandra said.

She seemed sad again and Penny hated to leave her. But she knew David had something important. Reaching across the small table, she squeezed Sandra's hand. "See you at three!" Her kind brown eyes looked into the sad dark ones of the unhappy girl.

Then something stirred deep in Sandra's mind and she managed a faint smile. "Sure."

"Nice to meet you, Sandra," David said, "and sorry I interrupted."

David turned and walked away. Penny followed him through the tables until they had left the eating area. He led her to the bridge, then asked for her camera. She was filled with questions but waited for him to explain.

"Mark's watching us from back there," David said quickly. "We saw something suspicious. I wanted to get you over here and then see if I could photograph someone behind you."

"That's a nice thing to say to a girl—you don't want

to take my picture. You want to take someone else's picture!" she scolded in mock disappointment.

"I've already taken half a dozen pictures of you with Mark's camera! But something's up." He hadn't intended to tell her that he'd been taking her picture and was glad he could hide behind the camera so she couldn't see his embarrassment!

Puzzled but cooperative, she stood where he asked her to and smiled when he began to frame the shot. Her camera was a single lens reflex with a powerful zoom lens. David adjusted it to serve as a telescope.

Then he positioned himself with Penny between him and the stocky man in dark clothes. David focused on a table right beside the man and then suddenly stepped half a foot to the side of Penny, snapped the shutter, and stepped quickly back! He hoped he hadn't made the man suspicious. He'd only taken a moment to take the picture, and this would be a great shot, magnified by the zoom lens, straight from the front!

The man had been completely fooled! He'd waited for David and Penny to start across the bridge before he followed. Looking around with great care, he hadn't seen the other boy. So he'd strolled casually onto the bridge. Halfway across, he stopped in his tracks. Directly ahead, David was taking his picture!

He cursed and quickened his step. *I'll grab that camera and smash that boy's nose,* he thought to himself.

Suddenly Mark's voice behind him called out, "David! How're you doing?"

Completely surprised, the scar-faced man turned to find Mark just a few feet behind, looking directly at him, camera in hand. Obviously the two boys were working this trap together!

"I'm fine, Mark!" David replied with a grin. "Just taking a picture of beauty and the beast."

CHAPTER 5

"DON'T FAIL!"

"**Y**ou blundering fool! How could you let them see you and actually take your picture!"

Schmidt was enraged. For the past five minutes, he'd been pouring out his wrath on the scar-faced man in the turtleneck sweater.

There was one other man in the dark room, but he said nothing. Lean with blond hair, he wore a dark jacket and grey trousers. The right side of his face was badly bruised, his nose was swollen, and his forehead marked with a red line from a very recent cut. Scrunched awkwardly in his chair, he favored a bruised left knee. He was also afraid.

"You're useless now!" Schmidt continued, glaring with suppressed fury at the man who stood before him. "Get back to the Ukraine at once—before the French police pick you up! Your papers are ready. They're in your mail box."

"But, sir," the terrified man replied. Stocky, power-fully built, he nevertheless quailed before Schmidt. "I've worked up to this assignment! I lost those kids when a crowd of tourists came into the area. When the tourists moved on, the boys were gone and I didn't see

29

the girl. That's when I rushed over to where they'd been sitting and almost ran into her. She was still there! I hid at once and didn't know they saw me."

He was clearly afraid of being sent back. "Then one of the boys joined her, and led her to the bridge, and took her picture. I didn't follow until they were halfway across the bridge, mostly hidden by other people. But when I was halfway over, they turned and photographed me before I could duck! I wasn't expecting it. My orders were not to get caught so I just walked past and ignored them. I came straight here." He looked desperate, as indeed he was.

"Well, you *did* get caught! Caught in their photographs. Now the police will be on your trail. Get out!"

With a last despairing look, the man left the room.

Schmidt turned, struggling to control his frustration and anger. He looked bleakly around the dingy room. Barely twelve feet square, the floor was covered by a thin, cheap, grey carpet. Dull, yellowed, partially ripped wallpaper surrounded a small desk and a few chairs. This was his office in Paris and he hated it!

He swung his heavy head in the other man's direction. "We lost a huge opportunity—and several good men—in Africa. We lost a huge opportunity—and a lot of men—in Egypt. Now this fool has alerted those kids and tipped off Daring and his crowd that they're being watched. This is the worst thing that could have happened!"

He paced the small dark room like a caged lion, his

heavy tread shaking the floor. A black-haired man with a receding hairline, he had huge shoulders and arms and a thick, powerful body. His face was large and wide, his ears long, and his bleak grey eyes burned at the other man through round, metal-framed glasses.

"The political catastrophes in Europe these past few years have destroyed much of what we've achieved in this century! But we won't be stopped. I refuse to give up! We've got to have funds for our organization even though our governments have wrecked much of it. This second buried tomb in Egypt can bring us that money."

He stopped his pacing, loomed directly before the battered man in the chair, and made a visible effort to control his anger. His voice grew quiet. The blond man watched him carefully as he continued.

"Listen! That Egyptian tablet in the Louvre was broken into three pieces. Our man was studying two of these and keeping Daring and Froede's men from getting to the third. But our spy's been caught and they now have access to those two stones. The third piece is in another part of the museum. They don't know about it yet. And that's the one that tells of another tomb, ninety kilometers north of the one we tried to rob! It's covered with sand like everything else on that bank of the Nile, and no one knows it's there." He glared down at the younger man.

He smacked his fist into his palm, his face coloring with anger once again. "But our man didn't get pictures of that third piece before he was caught! The stupid fool! Daring and Froede's translator will learn of it as he studies the two stones he has. Soon, very soon, he'll track down the third piece, just as we did, and read about the other tomb. Then the Egyptian government will guard that too, just as it's guarding the first one, and we'll lose millions of dollars!"

He flung his arms wide in unrestrained frustration, and began to pace the small room again. His powerful body strained against his dark suit as he moved with surprising grace for a man so heavy.

The blond man kept quiet. He'd once seen Schmidt deal with an agent who'd failed. He didn't want to be the next victim. His bruised face felt awful and his knee felt worse, but he didn't move an inch.

Suddenly the phone rang. Schmidt crossed the room with surprising speed and engulfed the receiver in his huge hand. A muscle twitched in his face as he listened quietly. Finally Schmidt replied, "We're not quitting. I need four more men."

He listened for another minute and then hung up. Sitting on the edge of the small desk, he faced the smaller man. His face was bleak. "You're getting another chance."

The blond-haired man let out a deep breath.

Schmidt continued. "Froede and Daring's translator has an office in the Louvre and works there every day. He locks up his place each night. The French are also guarding the area with plainclothesmen.

"But, so far, they're letting those three teenagers carry some of his work to their office building on la Rue Dante—just a short way from the river. We've tapped their phone, so we'll know when their translator finds the third tablet. He'll send pictures of it before he translates it—that's how he's worked before. When we hear him tell the men in the office he's sending over pictures of this third stone, we'll be ready to grab them."

Schmidt stood up. The other man struggled painfully to his feet. Schmidt reached out and put his hand on his shoulder. "Don't fail me *this* time," Schmidt said quietly.

"Thank you, sir," Hoffmann replied gratefully. "We'll get those pictures!"

Schmidt's heavy face was somber as he looked at the smaller man. "Stay out of sight. Don't let yourself or any of your men be seen like that fool I just sent home!"

"No, sir."

"You look awful!"

"Yes, sir."

CHAPTER 6

THE FIFTH DAY

"**D**o you realize it's only been five days since we got out of that Egyptian tomb!" Penny observed the next morning.

The three were sitting at their favorite outdoor cafe, drinking hot chocolate and eating fabulous French pastries. The boys had already ordered seconds. Half the tables around them were filled with customers enjoying another clear day. David had been reading his history of the Greek army trapped in Persia; Mark had been studying the guidebook; and Penny was taking pictures of pigeons and of the people who were feeding them.

"Five days!" David said. "Is that all? It seems like a month!"

He wore a light-colored polo shirt with grey trousers and was leaning back comfortably in his chair beside Penny. Mark sat to his left, busy polishing off the remnants of his pastry.

"We were in Egypt for less than a week!" Mark said.

"I was ready to come to Paris!" Penny countered. "But maybe we can visit Cairo on our way back home. I'd really like to see the shops."

She wore a white blouse and a light green skirt, white shoes, and had a white ribbon in her hair. David had been trying to sneak a picture of her with Mark's camera, but she hadn't turned away and so far he'd been unable to do it.

"I'd like to see some of the other temples," Mark said. "We could spend months there and not see all the ancient buildings and things." He finished the last bite and looked for the waiter, wondering when he'd bring that second pastry. "But there's so much Egyptian stuff in the Louvre, and we'll get to see that this next week. David's probably got some history lectures ready for us." He rolled his eyes at his sister with a pained expression.

"In fact," David agreed quickly, "I have! Let me tell you about—"

Penny interrupted him. "Here comes Sandra!" She watched the sad-looking girl approach them through the tables. "How about leaving for a couple of minutes so we can talk."

"Well, here we go again, getting kicked out of our seats. What we won't do to please women!" David complained.

"Penny!" Mark protested. "The waiter's about to bring us those pastries we ordered. You're not asking us to leave now!" He looked anguished.

"Just for a few minutes, Mark," Penny pleaded. "Honest! This girl's in real trouble, and she seems willing to talk with me about it. Just give us a few minutes.

I'll wave when you can come over. Please?"

"Oh, all right," Mark agreed. He looked across the table and his face brightened. "Hey! Take your time! Those beautiful girls just passed our table for the third time! They're looking David over. This is probably an evangelistic opportunity and we shouldn't miss it." He tried to sound pious as he got up. "Let's go, David. We shouldn't miss this chance to witness—after all, Penny's doing her part."

Penny's dark brown eyes showed alarm. "What girls are you talking about?"

Then she saw the two girls in high heels and short, tight skirts that had just passed, looking back at the boys with laughing eyes as they flounced to a nearby table and sat down.

"You stay away from them. They're not the right kind of girls and you know it, Mark!" Penny was clearly distressed.

"Aw, Sis, I'm only trying to do a good deed—just like you are with Sandra," Mark replied casually. "Let's go, David," he said. "Duty calls!"

"Mark!" Penny was alarmed.

"Hi!" Sandra said, stopping at their table. "Is it O.K. if I join you?"

"Sure it is," Mark said, smiling and holding out the chair for her.

Startled, she looked at him for a moment and then sat down. She was nervous.

"I'm so glad you could come back!" Penny said

warmly. "You remember Mark and David?"

"Excuse us for leaving, Sandra," Mark said in a friendly way. "David and I have a little chore to do. We'll be back soon." He looked at Penny. "See you later, Sis."

"Mark!" she said with some heat, looking anxiously up at David.

But then David winked at her, and nodded his head toward her brother as if to say, *Don't worry! He's just teasing you.*

Mark walked off, whistling a merry tune.

"Penny," David said quietly, "you know he wouldn't give the time of day to girls dressed like that—and neither would I." He looked at her for a moment. "We'll be back in a little while," he said as he turned and followed Mark.

Sandra was puzzled. "What's wrong with the way those girls are dressed?" she asked Penny.

Penny sighed and began to explain.

Another conversation was occurring several blocks away, only this one was by telephone. From the Louvre, Keno dialed the office of the international consortium for which Daring and Froede were working. "Is Mr. Daring there?" he asked. The excitement in his voice was obvious to the receptionist.

"I believe he is. Let me ring him," she replied.

In a minute Daring picked up the phone. "Daring here."

"Jim," Keno said, "we've found another tomb!"

"What do you mean, Keno?" asked Daring, completely mystified.

"We've found another tomb, Jim!" Keno repeated, his voice high with excitement. "The writing on the stones I was studying told of another building on the Nile. I asked the director for a complete inventory of the tablets in the Louvre. This list he gave me mentioned another piece broken off from the tablet in Cairo—one we didn't know about. I asked to see it. It tells of another tomb, north of the one we were exploring and built about the same time!" He paused. "Jim, this is stupendous! Two major finds along the Nile! Two undiscovered tombs! This is the archaeological event of the century!"

Daring was stunned. "Have you translated the stone?"

"Not completely, but enough to know the second tomb exists," Keno replied. "I'll send the pictures over this afternoon for your men to study. By tomorrow I'll have a rough translation."

"Very good, Keno," Daring replied. "I'll ask the kids to drop by this afternoon and pick up the pictures. Who would have thought we'd make discoveries like these? You've done a great job!"

"Thank you, Jim. Tell them to come by around 2 P.M. The pictures will be ready by then."

CHAPTER 7

THIS IS OUR PLAN!

Eight men were jammed uncomfortably into the small smoke-filled room in the basement of a building just off the Place Maubert, a short distance south of the Seine. The mobs that engulfed the open-air market held in the square on Tuesdays, Thursdays, and Saturdays provided excellent cover for the gang of thugs Hoffmann had assembled. They could move in and out of the area and not be noticed among such crowds.

Schmidt's organization had rented three adjoining rooms in the basement of the tall, narrow building. At both ends there were entrances to the streets above. The place had served Schmidt's men well for the past year, and it was serving them well now.

Hoffmann looked at the group. *What idiots!* he thought to himself. *Where are the real warriors we had a few years ago?* But he kept these thoughts to himself. This was the team he'd been given, and these were the men he would have to lead.

The two Germans he knew well. Eric, a blond giant
with pockmarked face and monstrous arms and shoulders, leaned against the back wall of the small room.
His rolled-back sleeves revealed the intricate tattoos
that covered his hamlike forearms. Dark shirt and
trousers made him look even more sinister.

The man beside him was smaller, but still over six
feet. Olaf's dark hair was greased straight back from
his forehead, and his face was deathly white. He too
was powerfully built, but more importantly he was an
expert in the martial arts. Dirty white pants and a dirty
white shirt made him look like a victim in a morgue.

The four Frenchmen were dockworkers and street
fighters. *Turtleneck sweaters, dark baggy slacks, thick
brutal faces, long noses—they all look like criminals*,
Hoffmann thought with disgust. But they could fight,
Schmidt had told him, and that was what mattered.

Two men from North Africa completed the crew.
Tall, slender, and quiet, they preferred to use knives
rather than their fists. Schmidt had warned them stern-
ly to avoid bloodletting unless it was ordered by
Hoffmann. In their dark, elegant suits they looked
completely out of place in the gang of thugs. Actually,
they could have been mistaken for bankers.

Hoffmann hated scratch teams, men thrown together
at the last minute, men who hadn't worked together
before. How he longed for the teams he'd trained so
carefully in East Germany! But as he looked them
over, he reminded himself that he had to hope for the

best. After all, these men were selected by Schmidt; they were clearly fighters; and there were enough of them to get the job done.

The six Europeans were smoking; Hoffmann coughed ominously. The men got the point and reluctantly put out their cigarettes. They looked at the man of middle height in front of them—face bruised on one side, forehead slashed by something, nose swollen, standing awkwardly to favor a very sore knee—and they sensed danger. Even the big men knew that Hoffmann was a man to fear, although only Eric and Olaf could tell them why.

"You've studied the map," Hoffmann reminded them. "You know the route these kids take. Our objective is to grab the case with the photographs. Probably the girl will be carrying it. Once again, this is how we'll do the job."

Again he went over the scheme. When they got word that the kids were bringing the photographs from the Louvre, the men would take their assigned positions. The four Frenchmen would be lounging by the bridge, in pairs, with some space between them. The two North Africans would be in the car, and Olaf and Eric would be at the corner. When the three kids reached the corner and turned toward their father's temporary office, the trap would be sprung!

The North Africans would drive the car up beside the three Americans, and the two Germans would grab the girl with her camera case or yank it from her. The nearest pair of Frenchmen would knock the boys aside, then block the way in front of and behind the car, screening off the action from the other pedestrians.

Hoffmann would be with the two Germans, ready to give the signal to attack, and lend a hand to any of the teams. They'd throw the camera case—or the girl with it, whichever was easier—into the car, while the remaining men would block the road temporarily. Then the car would take the girl or the case quickly to the warehouse.

"Once we have the pictures, you men will scatter," Hoffmann concluded. "The gendarmes won't reach this place until long after we're gone. Stay out of sight and don't surface until we tell you to! You'll be well paid."

"When?" one of the Frenchmen asked instantly, looking boldly at Hoffmann.

Hoffmann looked back quietly through steel-grey eyes. The man became nervous and dropped his gaze to the floor.

"Tomorrow," Hoffmann replied. He looked at each man in turn, sizing them up again. "Any questions?"

There were none.

CHAPTER 8

THE OUTDOOR CAFE

Mark and David strolled away from Penny and Sandra, weaving through the tables in the outdoor cafe and passing the flirtatious girls without a glance. Then they turned to the left and walked slowly around the outer tables, looking now and then at Penny, as they'd promised Mr. Daring they would.

"Did she tell you much about her talks with Sandra yesterday?" David asked, as they stepped carefully around two poodles lying by their owners' feet. "Frankly, I hate to leave her alone with the girl."

"So do I," Mark replied. "But she said last night that Sandra has been bumming around Europe with her boyfriend. He's the guy who got so mad yesterday and left her at the table."

"Looked like a jerk to me," David said.

"He is. They both dropped out of college, sold her car and whatever else they could, and caught a cheap flight to Europe. Her dad left her mom and the kids several years ago and tried to make up for it by sending her money."

"So that punk she's with took advantage of a girl without a father," David concluded, his face grim.

"You got it," Mark said. "Don't they always?"

David's face was sad. "If girls in those situations could just stay away from lousy guys until they grow up and find a decent man! Maybe Penny can help her wise up."

"Maybe," Mark replied doubtfully. "But she's hoping he'll come back before her money runs out."

They walked casually around the rim of the table area, keeping Penny in sight and enjoying the people from all over the world who walked past them. They didn't want to go too far from the second helpings of pastries that the waiter had just brought to their table.

"I can't wait to see the catacombs!" David said.

"Me neither! I never heard of a city with so much beneath it: miles and miles of subways, quarries, tombs, sewers, and the ancient catacombs. Did you know that the French Resistance had their main headquarters right under the city all through the Second World War?"

"I read that," David replied. "Penny's got our flashlights in her camera case. The guidebook says to take your own lights along on the tour."

Mark's broad face showed his puzzlement. "Frankly, I'm surprised Penny's willing to go underground again—after last week!"

David nodded. "I think Mr. Froede reassured her

when he said that Hoffmann was out of our lives forever. Besides, she's eager to see the old caves and catacombs."

"How in the world did Hoffmann just disappear from the earth like that?" Mark asked.

Before David could reply, Mark grabbed his arm. "She's waving us back! Now we can get those pastries!" Grinning, he struck out for the table where the girls were sitting. David followed just as eagerly.

Sandra got up and walked away before they reached the table. Penny's face was solemn when the boys sat down.

"Anything wrong?" David asked, looking after the departing girl and then back at Penny.

Penny's brown eyes were thoughtful, but she smiled brightly. "No. She's waiting for her father to wire her some money. She had to get back to the hotel. Her boyfriend's left her. I told her that was good riddance and that Dad would help if she needed it, but she said she'd get money from her father.

"I think she wants to get out of this situation," Penny continued, looking at Mark and David in turn. "But she doesn't know how. She's given herself to boys ever since her dad left several years ago, and she doesn't know anything else to do." Then her face reddened and she looked down. "She says all the girls she knows have done that."

"It sure hasn't made her happy," Mark observed, biting into the succulent chocolate pastry which was waiting for him. "Not if her face is any indication."

"Does it ever?" David asked. Then he looked up as two magnificent dogs approached. "Look at those dogs!" David marveled. "There're more dogs than people in this city."

Two huge Russian wolfhounds were passing by with their owners in tow. Beautiful in brown and white, they were an unusual sight. Their long bodies, deep chests, and small heads suggested their incredible speed and fighting instincts.

"Did you know there are *restaurants* for dogs in Paris?" Penny asked in amazement. "The waiters sit them up at the table, wrap napkins around their necks, and serve them their food—at the table!"

"What a country!" Mark observed. "Why don't we order seconds?" he asked innocently.

"That *was* seconds!" Penny replied. "Mark, you're going to stuff yourself to death if you're not careful."

"On those tiny little bites?" he protested. "Gosh, those plates must have been the ones they were supposed to give the little dogs."

"Not at this restaurant," Penny laughed. "This is for people!"

Just then Mr. Daring came up. "Eating again, Penny?" he asked in surprise. "You're going to lose your pretty figure if you don't stop swallowing Parisian pastries!" He sat down and smiled at her.

"Dad!" she protested. "It's these boys! I'm trying to keep them from wrecking their health!"

"Well, this will help. Keno's just called. He's got some pictures for you to take to the office. You can pick them up after lunch, and deliver them on your way to the catacombs. What time is the tour?"

"We can go at 2 P.M.," Penny replied. "We've got our flashlights. Don't you want to come? It should be exciting!" Her eyes were bright with the prospect of seeing the historic catacombs under the great city.

"Thanks, I can't make it today. But we'll meet you at the hotel before supper."

"Yes, sir," Mark answered confidently, "we'll be back in plenty of time for supper."

CHAPTER 9

"WE'VE GOT THEM SURROUNDED!"

Hoffmann had barely picked up the phone before he heard Schmidt's voice barking on the line. "They've got the pictures and they're on their way to Daring's office. Don't fail!" He hung up without waiting for an answer.

"No, sir," Hoffmann replied before he realized that the line was dead. Slamming down the receiver he yelled to Eric, "Signal the men! They're coming!"

The well-laid plan went smoothly into action. The North Africans were parked a block away, waiting for the signal. The four Frenchmen were asleep on their bunks in the next room. Olaf was at his station on the south side of the Pont-Neuf, the bridge the kids walked over on their trips from the Louvre to their father's temporary office in Paris.

Eric yelled to the Frenchmen in the next room to get up, and then called Olaf on the hand-held radio.

"The kids are coming! So are we."

Next he called the North Africans on another channel and alerted them. They started the engine of their parked car and prepared to move into position as soon as Olaf told them that the kids had crossed the bridge.

Eric and Hoffmann left the building first by the eastern exit and walked casually around the block before heading north to the bridge. The Frenchmen left in pairs from the other side of the building.

The various forces converged with silent purpose on the spot where the ambush would occur. The four Frenchmen and two Germans had to work around the crowds that packed the open-air market. They had practiced this, however, and it didn't interfere with their timing at all.

The North Africans also had to avoid the many vehicles that clogged the streets leading to the huge market. They too had practiced. They drove slowly along, hugging the curb as closely as possible, letting cars pass. They had to be near when the men grabbed Penny or her camera case.

Completely unaware of the sinister forces encircling them, Penny, Mark, and David strolled across the Pont-Neuf Bridge under a clear summer sky. Penny walked between the two boys and carried Keno's latest pictures of the Egyptian tablets in the camera case slung over her shoulder. Once over the bridge, the three turned left and walked along the Seine toward the Place St. Michel and their favorite restaurant.

"We've probably got time for one of those pastries before we deliver the photographs," Mark said hopefully.

"Mark, you've stuffed yourself already! We've got no time to spare if we're going to give Dad the pictures, then make the two-o'clock tour of the catacombs," Penny replied. She wondered what excuse he'd think of next!

David laughed at their banter. Actually, they were all looking forward to the tour of the catacombs, and not even Mark wanted to miss it.

They strode along, increasing their pace, breathing the fresh air, and enjoying the peaceful bustle of the street along the famous river. Small boats passed, and the teenagers were absorbed by the beauty and interest of the scene. Arriving at the Rue LaGrange, they were about to turn right as usual.

"Let's keep going and try another street," David said suddenly on impulse. "There's a street three blocks ahead that we've never tried. We may be missing a lot of Paris by going the same way everytime."

"That's fine with me," Mark answered, always eager for new sights.

So they walked on past the Rue LaGrange and several more as well. They turned right on the Rue de Bievre.

Olaf spoke frantically into his radio. "They didn't turn! They're going on!"

Hoffmann got the message and cursed. "Eric, call

the Africans. Tell them to listen to Olaf and adjust their position."

Hoffmann himself changed channels and called the one Frenchman out of the four who had a radio. The Frenchman acknowledged the message, waved to the two men forty yards behind, nudged his companion, and moved along the river. They were across the street from the three teenagers and paralleled their path.

Hoffmann directed the teams as they adjusted to the new directions. Soon his groups were moving smoothly in their new paths to enclose the three kids against the river. The minute the Americans crossed the street, the plan would go into action.

"They've got to turn right soon, if they're going to Daring's office!" Olaf complained in his radio.

"Don't worry," Hoffmann replied. "We know that they're carrying the pictures we want. They'll turn. When they do, we'll have them trapped in a narrower street and it will be all the easier for us We've got them surrounded!" he exulted.

The kids walked along the bustling riverbank. Across the river to their left was the famous Isle de la Cite, the original site of the huge city of Paris. Flocks of pigeons flew overhead; numerous people fished peacefully on the banks of the river; couples walked hand in hand along the bank; and little children played as they followed their parents who strolled along the riverside.

"Isn't Paris wonderful!" Penny exclaimed, her eyes shining with pleasure. David grinned back.

She smiled up at David, and he thought for the hundredth time that day that she was the prettiest girl he'd ever seen. She carried the burgundy camera case over her left shoulder. The three of them were bantering and laughing as they walked vigorously along the famous riverside.

Across the street, to their right, about twenty yards ahead of them, two burly Frenchmen in working clothes clumped along the sidewalk, unlit pipes clamped in their mouths. About the same distance behind Mark, Penny, and David, also across the street, two other thugs were following. Olaf was ahead of all of them while the North Africans followed slowly in the dark green sedan. Hoffmann and Eric were winding their way along narrow streets a block to the right of the river.

The plan was intact. Hoffmann wasn't worried. Those pictures were as good as in his hands!

"We've got them surrounded," he repeated to himself. His battered face, swollen nose, and brightly scarred forehead contrasted strangely with his trim figure and dark suit. Those passing by gave him a second glance. Eric walked beside him, his menacing bulk forcing people to give way.

"That's the street," David pointed. "We've never tried it, but the map shows that it leads to the market, which is right on our way."

"I can take some great pictures from that narrow street," Penny exclaimed, as they stood on the curb and waited for the traffic to pass.

"Not too many," Mark reminded her. "We don't want to miss the tour of the catacombs."

"What if I stop long enough to photograph you buying a chocolate pastry at the market?" she asked slyly, her eyes laughing at him.

"Now you're talking! We've got plenty of time for that!"

"Let's go," David said, as a gap in the cars appeared. Quickly they crossed the street and started down the Rue de Bievre toward the market.

"Gosh!" Mark observed. "There's a bunch of hand-carts and wagons ahead of us. Guess they're going to the market too."

"Look at those folks," David said suddenly. "I bet they're from Turkey."

A large group of dark-clothed men followed by veiled women in very long dresses came towards them, striding past a cart piled high with tomatoes. A gang of children clustered around the women.

Olaf, leaning against a building at the corner of the Rue de Bievre, had picked the right street. As soon as he saw the three Americans cross the road and head down the narrow way, he radioed the other teams. Then he followed his prey, moving with a smooth grace that contrasted sharply with his dirty and unkempt appearance.

The pair of Frenchmen across the street and ahead of the kids turned back toward the Rue de Bievre. The two Frenchmen following behind hurried along the river, catching up, while the sedan moved slowly beside them. All prepared to take the street the Americans had taken.

A short block south of all the others, Hoffmann and Eric increased their pace and entered the street, moving swiftly to close the trap. The three Americans were caught.

Through a gap in the crowd Hoffmann suddenly saw them.

"There they are!" he exulted into his small hand radio. "We've got them! Execute!" Switching off the machine, he jammed it into his coat pocket and moved swiftly after the giant Eric.

But someone else had been looking through that gap in the crowd.

"Mark!" Penny cried in alarm, stopping suddenly. "That's Hoffmann!"

CHAPTER 10

THE TRAP IS SPRUNG!

The magnificent pair of brown and white wolfhounds led their elegantly dressed masters through the hordes of people walking near the crowded open-air market. People who saw the large beasts gave them a wide berth.

Olaf never saw them. He was watching the three teenagers when they stopped suddenly, darted to their left to cross the street, then began running toward him and away from Hoffmann and Eric.

The master of martial arts in dirty white shirt and pants responded instantly. Pocketing his radio, he stepped smoothly from the curb and moved with deadly grace to intercept the kids, his vicious face wreathed in a sinister smile.

He gave little attention to the Turks walking leisurely from the market toward the river Seine. Led by two giant, darkly dressed men, the group included heavily veiled women in long dresses, carrying baskets of fresh food. A flock of children clustered around the adults, chattering loudly.

The deadly master of martial arts, two hundred and twenty pounds of lethal force, roughly knocked aside the woman in front of him and slammed into the one-hundred-and-fifteen-pound male wolfhound!

The instincts of the breed took over immediately. The magnificent animal snapped his long head to the side and gripped Olaf's thigh in his powerful jaws.

The karate master screamed in pain as he fell to the street, his left hand striking toward the animal's head even as his right knee hit the ground. The wolfhound released his bite and caught Olaf's hand as it flashed down, crushing the bones in his long mouth.

Olaf screamed again, scrambled to his feet, and stumbled back from the animal which was finally under the control of its astonished master. Staggering backward, Olaf tripped over the female dog. She bit deeply into his other leg.

Yelling again, Olaf tumbled forward. Trying desperately to keep balance, the deadly karate master crashed into the largest of the Turkish women with his arms outstretched in what appeared to be a flying tackle.

She shrieked and brought the basket of three dozen eggs smashing down on his head as she fell to the ground under his charge.

The other wives screamed in alarm, the children cried out, and the astonished Turkish men turned to see one of their women screaming on the ground under the body of a large European man.

Yelling with rage, the Turks charged. The desperately hurt Olaf struggled to his feet, head covered with a mass of yellow egg yolk and broken shell, cursing with helpless anger as he tried to claw the flowing mess from his eyes.

The master of martial arts never had a chance. The Turkish phalanx hit him with the velocity only anger at violence done to their women could generate, and the man covered with raw egg went down under the charge. Pounding him madly, the Turks proceeded to make pulp of the once-deadly karate master.

Seeing Olaf go down, Eric yelled and charged. Hoffmann, watching his plans dissolve in this totally unexpected riot, ran after him. The monstrous Eric crashed into the crowd of Turks, who rose from the body of the now-unconscious Olaf to meet this new threat.

Knocking two men aside with his fists, Eric attacked the largest Turk, a giant as large as he, with murderous intent.

Eric's foot slipped in a mess of broken egg; he stumbled forward, frantically trying to keep his balance, just as the Turk stepped neatly aside. The huge German crashed facedown onto a wheeled cart piled high with fresh tomatoes, and the cart lurched forward under his weight.

The outraged Turks raced after the moving vehicle, pounding the man spread-eagled on its top. Eric struggled to get up, but the gang of ferocious, yelling men ran alongside, beating him on the back and pushing him deeper into the pulpy tomatoes.. One of the men ripped away the leather wallet strapped to Eric's belt as they ran.

Then the vengeful Turks saw other possibilities than killing the infidel who'd attacked one of their women. Yelling in words their frenzied victim couldn't understand, they called out their plan as they chased the cart with its helpless cargo toward the river.

Faster and faster they ran, the tomato-covered Eric screaming in helpless rage from the racing wagon. Crowds of surprised people scattered like chickens before a raiding fox as the strange procession tore through their midst.

Hoffmann ran behind, raging and wildly clubbing one of the Turks as he caught up with the charging group inexorably hurtling toward the river.

But he was too late to save Eric from his fate. The cart shot toward the river. The gang of men around it lifted it easily over the curb to propel it swiftly on its way. The vehicle catapulted over the edge of the bank and plunged to the water below, Eric still aboard.

Hoffmann skidded to a stop—too late again! The outraged Turks turned, saw another enemy, and charged. Hoffmann spun on one foot as the other shot out with deadly accuracy. A big Turk went down on the street, tripping another who charged just behind him. The others followed and smothered Hoffmann in their assault. The uninjured side of his face was smashed by a mighty fist, his arms and legs grabbed by four men, and his body propelled out over the bank in a mighty arc. Yelling as he soared, his arms flailed helplessly and his body twisted in its flight to the Seine. The battered man slammed into the dirty river below.

Hearing but not seeing the riot behind them, Mark, Penny, and David ran frantically up the street toward the river. They skidded around the building on the corner and dashed directly into two French dockworkers who were running toward the yelling crowd of Turks. But as they passed, the Frenchmen recognized the three Americans.

Cursing madly, the two shabbily clad men halted their charge, turned, and shot after the youngsters who'd rounded the corner and were now out of sight. The shorter of the two men in pursuit knocked over a young mother wheeling her baby in a carriage. The woman screamed as she went down while the carriage rolled on out of control.

Four Belgian nuns in their long grey robes and stiffly starched headdresses watched with astonishment as the three youngsters ran past. But they gasped in shock as they saw one of the pursuing Frenchmen knock down the young mother.

The two younger nuns raced to grab the rolling baby carriage, while one of the older ones ran to help the frightened but uninjured mother. But the other nun, a statuesque Amazon of a woman, deftly slipped the strap of her heavy black leather bag from her shoulder,

pivoted on one foot so that she stood in a classic bat-
ter's stance, swung her torso smoothly, and—with the
grace and power of a major league player—smashed
the bag into the stomach of the oncoming Frenchman.
Stunned, he doubled over and crashed to the ground as
the breath whooshed out of him.

The victorious Turks walked back down the tomato-
reddened street, laughing and retrieving their wounded.
The one who'd taken Eric's wallet whistled at the roll
of franc notes it contained. Then the owner of the
tomato cart rushed toward them, waving his arms in
outrage, demanding his cart. Peeling off a wad of the
franc notes, the grinning Turk handed him payment
enough for several carts. The Frenchman whistled at
the amount of money, took it greedily, laughed and
thanked the Turks.

Hoffmann's plan had dissolved!

CHAPTER 11

THE FORCES
REASSEMBLE

Mark, Penny, and David raced down the sidewalk, weaving among surprised passersby.

"Who were those guys?" Mark called.

"I never saw them before," David answered. "They just turned when we passed them and took off after us."

He looked over his shoulder again. "I don't see Hoffmann or that big guy he was with."

Penny ran ahead, with Mark and David forming a protective wall behind her.

"They're slowing down, Mark," David observed, looking back again.

"Did you notice a green car that's moving with them?" Mark asked.

"Yeah. What do you think they want?"

"Us—or Penny's camera case," Mark said urgently to David. "They must be after those pictures Keno gave her to take to Dad. Why else would anyone be chasing us? After all, they are with Hoffmann."

"That must be it," David agreed. Then he saw a way out. "Look. A taxi stand! Let's grab one! Penny, in the taxi. Quick!"

They ran to the first taxi in line and jumped in. Mark called out to the driver, "Rue des Ecoles!" He continued in careful French, "We're in a hurry! There's a hundred francs in it for you if we get there fast!"

The taxi roared away from the curb and dashed down the street, weaving around the slower cars.

Behind them, the three Frenchmen stopped their chase along the sidewalk.

"They've taken a taxi!" one shouted. "Quick, Pierre, get in the car with the Africans. We'll take a taxi and follow the one ahead. You follow us, but stay back so they don't see you!"

Pierre ran over to the green sedan that moved along the street beside them, waved it to a stop, and jumped in. The other two men piled in a taxi, offered the driver a fistful of francs, and told him to follow the taxi just ahead.

But a bus moved in front of them before they could pull out from the curb, and for a few minutes they couldn't even see the taxi with the kids. The men cursed in frustration, but the driver spoke up. "Don't worry," he told them. "When the taxi turns, I'll see it."

He was right. Two blocks later the taxi with the three Americans turned to the right. The three Americans inside hadn't noticed the taxi following them.

Mark, Penny, and David had begun to relax. "The bus blocked us from their sight," David said as he glanced out the back window. "Now we can get these pictures to your dad's office."

They looked back repeatedly, but never saw the green sedan. It was a long way back, just in sight of the pursuing taxi.

"I guess we shook 'em," Mark observed with relief. His broad face broke into a grin. "What a surprise!"

"How can Hoffmann have followed us *here?*" Penny asked, astounded.

"We think he may be after those pictures Keno gave us to deliver to Dad," Mark said thoughtfully. "Hoffmann tried to steal the treasures from pharaoh's tomb last week, but he failed. I bet that's why he's followed Dad and Keno to Paris. He knows they're on to something else that could bring him a lot of money."

"Gosh!" she exclaimed. "And we thought he was out of our lives forever!"

"Yeah," Mark agreed.

'Well, your father will know how to get police protection for the work Keno's doing," David said confidently. "And the company they're working for can have the police look for Hoffmann. He's wanted in Egypt, you know. Once we deliver these pictures to Keno, Hoffmann really will be out of our lives."

Back at the river, Hoffmann had come to the surface spluttering. Battered from his encounter with the Turks, he was completely mystified by the riot that had wrecked his carefully laid plans. *What went wrong?* he asked himself, even as he floundered in the filthy water.

Then he saw the boat approaching. *Rescue!* he thought. Swiftly he swam toward it. The boat, with a husband and wife aboard, crossed over from the other bank and cut the motor beside the feebly swimming Hoffmann. The man, a middle-aged fisherman in grey shirt and black beret, reached strong arms over the side of the boat, grabbed Hoffmann, and hauled him in. He flopped on the wooden deck, drenched, sore, and very confused.

The kindly man handed him a towel. Struggling to sit up, Hoffmann took the rough cloth and rubbed his dripping hair. He started to dry his face, but stopped when his bruised skin screamed with pain.

Looking around almost in a daze, he saw that these people were obviously friendly. He took out the small radio from his inside pocket, swiftly took it apart, and methodically began to dry each piece with the towel they'd given him. He was desperate to know if the thing would still work.

The couple looked wonderingly at the miniaturized electronic wizardry.

"I'm from the police," Hoffmann explained, in fluent and rapid French. He continued with a string of lies that came easily to the practiced criminal. "A gang of Turks attacked a Frenchman and his wife as they sold tomatoes in the market. My assistant and I were passing by, and when we went to help our countrymen, the Turks attacked us and threw us in the river. I've got to call for help."

Outraged at the indignities perpetrated against this nice policeman, the couple nodded wisely, thankful that they might have some small part in righting this injustice perpetrated by lawless foreigners.

Swiftly Hoffmann reassembled the radio; then he called the Africans in the green sedan.

The machine worked! Hoffmann recognized the voice of the man beside the driver who answered with great relief. "Where did you go? We're following those Americans—they've taken a taxi."

"You mean you let them get away!" Hoffmann swore in fluent French, as the enormity of his situation sank in upon him. How would he face Schmidt if he failed to get those pictures?

"They ran past the Frenchmen. There was nothing we could do!"

Hoffmann's tired mind struggled to collect itself and salvage something from this catastrophe.

"Wait!" the African said, interrupting Hoffmann's tortured thoughts. "They're getting out. They're going into the office that Daring is using."

"Don't let them see you!" Hoffmann commanded.

"We won't," the African assured him.

Just then the Frenchman called from the taxi. "We've just gone past them, and we're circling the block. We'll wait for them at the corner if you want."

"No! Go back to the house at once. We've got to reassemble."

Then he ordered the Africans in the sedan to return to the bridge and pick him up. "I'm on a boat," he concluded.

"On a boat!" the African replied, shocked. "How did that happen?"

"Never mind how it happened." Hoffmann struggled to control himself in front of the old couple. He tried to maintain the air of an honest French policeman. "Just return and pick me up at the Pont l'Archeveche. Understand?" He had to collect the group and make plans to get those pictures!

"All right," the African said.

Hoffmann sat back, thinking. He'd lost Eric, somehow. He'd lost Olaf. But he had the Frenchmen and the Africans. And he still had the man listening in on the phone in Daring's office. There had to be a way to get those pictures!

He turned to the French couple, told them how helpful they'd been to the forces of justice, and how he planned to arrest the violent foreigners. The simple fisherman and his wife were immensely pleased.

Then Hoffmann asked them if they'd let him off at the bridge just ahead, where an undercover agent would pick him up and take him to headquarters. They gladly agreed, thrilled and honored to be part of France's fight for justice.

But behind the facade, Hoffmann's mind was in turmoil. What had caused the riot that destroyed his careful plan? How would he get the pictures of the

Egyptian tablet now that those kids had taken them to their father's office? Had he failed again?

CHAPTER 12

A CHANGE OF PLANS

The taxi screeched to a stop in front of the office building. Mark shoved a fistful of francs toward the grateful driver, and the three dashed across the sidewalk and into the entrance.

"I don't think we were followed," David said as they climbed the steep stairs in the narrow, grey stairwell.

"We must have lost them," Penny replied gratefully.

"I bet we did," Mark added. "But what a surprise! Hoffmann!"

"And just five days after Uncle Paul said that we'd never see him again!" Penny exclaimed.

"Where in the world did he come from?" David asked. "How did he get away from the Egyptian army?"

Then they were at the third-story landing. Turning into the hall, they walked rapidly toward Mr. Daring's temporary office.

The secretary informed them he wasn't there, and they asked for Mr. Daring's assistant, Mr. Dubois. In a minute, he appeared. A heavyset man in a dark suit with metal-rimmed glasses and friendly smile, he had been temporarily assigned to Daring from the French branch of the corporation.

Penny took the pictures from her camera case and handed them to him.

"We think someone is after these!" she told him anxiously. "We were chased by some men on the way here, but we lost them. One of them was Hoffmann, the leader of the gang that tried to rob the temple in Egypt. Can you keep the pictures safe?"

"Certainly," he assured her, as he took them from her. "We'll put them in our safe. Then I'll call the police. Can you three identify the men who chased you?"

"We can identify some of them," David replied. Penny and Mark nodded.

"Good!" He immediately called the police, spoke in very rapid French which Mark and Penny could barely follow, and put down the receiver. "They're sending someone at once."

Thirty minutes later the three walked out of the office to the street, having told the police all they could about the men who had chased them. Mark and Penny hadn't been able to reach their parents, though they had called several times.

"I guess we should take that tour of the catacombs tomorrow," Mark said, obviously disappointed.

"Well, Mr. Dubois said the caves are cold, and that we'd need sweaters. There's no sense freezing!" Penny replied.

"She's right, Mark," David added. "We can go see the catacombs tomorrow. Let's go back to the restaurant and wait for your folks."

"Oh, you two are just looking for excuses to stuff yourselves again! And you thought we were going to starve in this country!" Penny taunted.

They hailed a taxi and Mark directed the driver to the cafe.

Back at the river, four gendarmes had driven up in a Jeep and rushed to rescue the man they'd been told was drowning in the Seine.

Eric, blind with rage, had found a series of rough projections in the stone bank and gotten himself halfway up by the time the police arrived. Leaning over the bank, they called down to him. The dripping man looked up and saw four uniformed heads peering at him. Shocked at the realization that he might soon be questioned by police, he let go his rocky handhold and fell back into the river. Coming to the surface, he began to swim rapidly across to the other side.

Outraged at this action, the police who'd come to rescue him jumped in their Jeep and raced across the bridge. Slamming to a stop, they jumped out of the Jeep, ran to the edge of the bank, and waited for the big man to climb up.

Laboriously Eric pulled his battered and bruised body up the steep bank. Painfully he clambered over the top. Then he caught his breath for a minute as he rested on his hands and knees, head hanging down in exhaustion, water pouring from his huge frame.

"Come with us, monsieur!" the sergeant said.

Eric looked up. Four policemen were standing before him, and they were not happy.

"I don't need any help," he replied in passable but not fluent French.

"We'll give it anyway, monsieur," the sergeant replied firmly, nodding to his men. Two of them went to Eric, grabbed his arms, and helped the giant to his feet where he stood swaying feebly. But his brain was racing. He had to get away from the police!

They led him to the Jeep, and put him in the back with a policeman on each side.

Panic-stricken, Eric began to plead with the sergeant to release him. "I'm just a tourist!" he protested. "I fell in the river by mistake!"

"That's not what twenty Turkish workers have said, monsieur," the sergeant replied. "They have serious charges. They say that you and a friend of yours assaulted their women."

"What! They're crazy!" Frantic now with fear and rage, he lurched over the man to his left.

Cursing, the policeman fell forward under the blow of Eric's powerful knee, striking the head of the driver in front of him. The driver's body was knocked into the wheel. He struggled to regain control and jerked the wheel suddenly to the left.

The Jeep swerved violently, barely avoided a cab,

bounced over the curb, and soared off the bank. Eric was fighting to free himself from the grip of a police-man when the vehicle dove into the river.

Meanwhile, the remnants of Hoffmann's team had returned to their quarters. The two impeccably dressed North Africans, the three brutal French dockworkers, and Hoffmann were all that returned. Utterly dejected, they tried to reconstruct what had happened to ruin their fine plans.

Hoffmann's face was a wreck. Battered on both sides now, his nose bloodied again and swollen, he felt as though he'd been run over by a train.

He'd changed into dry clothes and was sitting mis-erably before the survivors who were slouched around the room. They'd placed a call to the police station, calling from a public phone so they could not be traced to their apartment, and learned that Olaf, Eric, and the shorter Frenchman were all behind bars.

"The man at the desk was eager to question me about how I knew them," the taller of the two Africans told Hoffmann, "but I hung up."

"Are they being held on any charges?" Hoffmann asked, sick at heart by the news of another disaster. These kids had defeated him at every turn!

"I don't know. The police don't have to have charges in France. But he did say that they had assault-ed people in the streets and would be interrogated. One of the Germans attacked a Turkish woman, and the Frenchman attacked a young mother, or so he said."

"Does anyone know what actually *happened?*" Hoffmann's rage made him nearly incoherent. "One minute we were all closing in on them, and the next there was chaos! I saw Olaf down under a crowd of Turks; then Eric was thrown on a cart and run into the river." Hoffmann wondered if he were going mad. "How could this happen?" he shouted.

But no one could answer. The two Africans had been in the sedan along the river, and the Frenchmen had been walking along the same street. They'd all heard Olaf's signal, then Hoffmann's, and that was when everything fell apart.

"We've got to get our story together before Schmidt calls and demands an explanation," Hoffmann said frantically.

The sudden ringing of the phone startled them all.

Hoffmann jumped, blood draining from his bruised and bloodied face. The other men were staring at him.

The phone rang again. With a shaky hand and a fearful heart, he reached to pick it up.

CHAPTER 13

THE DANGER'S PAST NOW!

Later that night, Mark, Penny, and David were eating with Mr. and Mrs. Daring at a small restaurant. They'd been there before, and Penny had asked that they return. She loved the food and the atmosphere—the tablecloths, the candles, the waiters, the dark wood paneling of the walls.

"This place is marvelous!" she said to her dad. "Thanks for bringing us here!"

"You're welcome, Penny," he replied. "I love to see you and your mom enjoy the place."

Penny wore a dark blue dress with white beads around her neck and white earrings. David had been trying not to look at her too often. But every time he did, she smiled her wonderful smile, so he risked Mark's knowing grin repeatedly.

Their discussion turned to the exciting events of that day. Mr. Daring was puzzled by the story they'd told him.

"I can't imagine how Hoffmann got here," he said

wonderingly. "Paul Froede assured me that the Egyptians scouted the area where he was last seen and found no sign of him or of the Jeep he was driving. Both just vanished. And now, he's in Paris—and chasing the pictures of that Egyptian tablet!"

"What's in the pictures, Dad?" Penny asked eagerly. "Have you developed them yet?"

"In fact, we have!" her father replied. He glanced around cautiously and lowered his voice. "And you won't believe it—there's another tomb buried under the sand just north of the one you three explored last week!"

He looked at the three youngsters to see the effect of the news. Penny and the boys were stunned and so was his wife.

"Another tomb?" Mark asked.

"That's right. The tablet in the Louvre describes another tomb built at the same time, and tells of its location. Remember that whole part of the country was buried under sand dunes a couple of thousand years ago. That's why no one's ever found these buildings. But Hoffmann's people must have learned about it, and they may be trying to locate and rob it too."

"Just who is behind Hoffmann, Mr. Daring?" David asked, putting down his fork. "He's chased us first to Egypt and now to Paris."

"He's really pursuing everything our company does, David," Mr. Daring replied. "And he's connected with a unit of the former East German Secret Police. They were always an ally of the Soviet KGB. They all have remnants intact in Europe and throughout the world. Many of their people feel powerless with all the recent changes in their governments. They seem to be desperate for money to finance their continued operations. They're after us simply because our firm's on to some big money."

"But, Jim," his wife replied, a frown of concern on her face, "will there be no end to this harassment?"

"Well, Carolyn, I think we've got them," he said confidently. "The police caught three of the gang today—two Germans and a Frenchman, and the rest have scattered. The photographs are safe. Furthermore, we know what's in them, and we know where to find that second tomb. Hoffmann's team can't get the photos now, so I see no cause to worry about the men who got away."

He looked at the three young people as he sipped the marvelous French coffee. "I can't think of any reason they'd be after you any more. But just to be safe, I'll have our security guard pick up Keno's photos each day and leave you kids out of it. You can just avoid Keno's office and enjoy Paris."

"But what about Hoffmann, Dad?" Penny asked. "He's the one who turns up everywhere we go." It was uncanny, she thought, how Hoffmann kept appearing!

"That's true," he admitted. "And the police haven't found him yet, but there's an alert out for him. And he can't get the pictures from you now. I think he must know he's lost again," he said confidently.

"Incidentally," he interrupted their thoughts, "this

place is famous for its chocolate desserts. I know Penny's on a diet, but the rest of you might want to sample what they've got."

"I am *not* on a diet!" she protested hotly. "And you know I love chocolate!"

He looked carefully at her slender form in the chair beside him. "Sure you haven't put on a few pounds in this city?"

"I have not and you can't talk me out of dessert, Dad." She smiled at her father.

"O.K.," he agreed with a laugh and waved to the waiter.

Less than a mile away from the hotel where the Darings were staying, others were discussing Penny as well.

"There's no other way!" Schmidt spoke into the phone with such vehemence that Hoffmann, on the other end, recoiled. "You will capture that girl and hold her until Daring agrees to give us the pictures—all the pictures, and *all* the negatives—and two days for us to get the loot out of it! Do you understand?"

This was Schmidt's second call. In the first, he'd asked about the capture of the camera case with the pictures. Hoffmann cringed when he remembered that conversation!

Now Schmidt was giving orders. "You'll use the three Frenchmen and the two Africans. Capture the girl, hide her in your apartment, and I'll contact Daring."

"Yes, sir," Hoffmann replied.

"Those three kids are going to take a tour of the Paris catacombs tomorrow afternoon," Schmidt continued. "We've listened in on the phone conversations from Daring's office. Your men will join that tour. Those catacombs mesh with miles of underground tunnels and to hundreds of entrances to the basements of houses. We'll give you a map tomorrow morning, showing where you can grab the girl and rush her into one of the tunnels. Barricade the door behind you and take her above ground to a taxi, then to your place."

Hoffmann chewed his lower lip. The French government was especially hard on kidnappers, but Schmidt was harder on subordinates who disobeyed.

"Yes, sir." His face, bruised on both sides, felt awful. So did his swollen nose.

"The catacombs are very narrow in places," Schmidt continued. "Your men can block off the two boys and grab the girl easily. We'll study the map and find the best door to an exit tunnel for you. Duck through the door we select, block it behind you, and you'll be in the clear."

Sounds easy—on the phone! Hoffmann thought to himself. When would he ever escape the clutches of this man?

"Yes, sir, we'll do it."

"You'd better, Hoffmann." The line went dead as Schmidt hung up.

CHAPTER 14

TO THE CATACOMBS!

The next morning Mark, Penny, and David took a breathtaking tour of the Hotel de Cluny. Called a hotel, it was in fact a fabulous museum. Parts of the place had been constructed many centuries before.

"This thing is built right over a second-century Roman bath!" David told them. "And the ruins next door were the palace of the Emperor Julian. They called him 'Julian the Apostate' because he renounced Christianity and tried to exterminate it. He'd been badly treated by so-called *Christian* leaders, and became a sincere convert to ancient Roman paganism. But as he was dying, he realized that those pagan values couldn't hold society and families together. And he knew he'd failed."

"I think the Unicorn Tapestry is the most beautiful thing I've ever seen," Penny said, her brown eyes shining. "Imagine! No one knows how they made those dyes. It's a lost art that can't be matched today!" She was speaking about the incredible woven cloths they'd seen in the adjoining rooms: ancient tapestries of amazing workmanship. The Unicorn Tapestry pictured a medieval lady looking at herself in a mirror while a unicorn watched. People came from all over the world to see the historic piece of art.

"Oh, I wish I could take pictures of this place!" she exclaimed.

"But you wouldn't want to lug your camera through the catacombs, Penny," Mark reminded her. "You were wise to leave it at the hotel. We can come back here tomorrow."

"I thought the heads of the kings were awesome," David added. He'd been struck by the statues of twenty-one heads of former kings.

"Even without their noses?" Mark laughed.

"Even without their noses," David affirmed.

"What happened to their noses?" Penny asked as she moved her sweater from one hand to the other. They all wore warm pants and shirts, and carried sweaters for the coming visit to the cool catacombs.

"The mobs cut them off in the Revolution," David answered. "They tried to destroy everything that was Christian—statues, churches, everything. They hated the monarchy, so they mutilated the statues of kings they found in the churches."

"Yeah," Mark agreed grimly, "they hated the monarchy and killed the king, and then they got the tyranny that follows almost every revolution. Extermination squads using the guillotine, rule by a brutal elite, and more tyranny."

"That's right," David said. "Except for the American Revolution, that's what most people get from revolutions. The revolutionaries promise liberty but they deliver tyranny. Look what the Communists did in Russia and Europe, and all over the world!"

They wandered into the Baths, the largest remaining Roman vault in all of France. David was reading the guidebook as they walked, sharing its contents with Mark and Penny. He stopped to look up at the masonry above them.

"Do you realize this ceiling is *eighteen centuries old!*" he exclaimed in wonder. "How could it have lasted so long?"

"Especially after one of the medieval abbots shoveled eight feet of dirt on top of it for his garden!" Mark added. "They didn't know this Roman building was underneath!" Mark added.

"How do we know it'll last through the day?" Penny asked with a grin. "Maybe we better get out while we still can!"

But she wasn't about to leave, especially when they wandered to the upstairs gallery and saw the spectacular jewels and crowns. Light shone from the marvelously crafted gold and jewels, sending glorious colors in all directions. The three of them moved, lost in wonder, from display to display. The boys had a hard time prying Penny loose.

They spent all morning in the fabulous place, hardly

noticing the passage of time, enjoying the trip into history, the pleasant day, and the freedom from any threat of danger.

"We'd better get some lunch before we head for the catacombs," David reminded them.

So it was that they found themselves again at their cafe, watching the natives and tourists go by, the endless procession of dogs walking on leashes, and the waiters bringing marvelous food.

In a short while, Mr. Daring joined them. Dressed casually in slacks and sweater, he pulled out a chair and sat beside Penny, putting his arm around her shoulder. Mark waved the waiter over and they all ordered.

"Not going to the office today, Dad?" Penny asked.

"Not today, Penny," he replied. "Your Mom's shopping with some friends, and I'm meeting Keno for a tour of the universities."

He changed the subject. "Did you folks know that this city is probably the intellectual center of the world? There are around two hundred thousand students in the Paris universities on any given day, thousands and thousands of them from foreign lands. Forty-two nations in the world have French as either their first or second language, and these countries send their students and graduates to Paris."

He shook his head as he pondered the city's importance. "There's probably not a city on earth where there's a greater need for Christian influence and values—nor one with less idea of biblical truth. I just learned that there are sixty-five thousand registered astrologers in the Paris area. That's more than twice the number of Roman Catholic priests in the whole country! What a place for a Christian study center."

He looked over at Mark and Penny. "Maybe you two would want to spend some time here in a few years, doing graduate study. You know the language and a lot of the literature. Educated Frenchmen won't listen to a Christian witness from anyone who doesn't know their literature and their philosophy."

They continued chatting as they ate lunch. Then Mr. Daring began to describe the company that had hired him to do the preliminary engineering on the site in Egypt.

"Remember to thank the firm for the vacation you're enjoying!" he reminded them. "For a starter, you can write Paul Froede a letter."

"I'll write the letter, Dad, and then show the boys where to mark their Xs," Penny volunteered.

They finished their lunch, and the youngsters got up and left for the tour of the catacombs. None of the three noticed the powerfully built African in slacks and sweater who joined Mr. Daring after they left the table. He pulled out the chair where Mark had been and sat down. Daring grinned a welcome.

"Henri, if you'll just keep your eyes on them this afternoon, I'll be grateful. I wouldn't let them loose if we weren't sure that Hoffmann's gang is scattered. He's got no reason now for bothering them. But I will feel better knowing someone from police security is taking that tour with them."

"It's my pleasure, Jim," Henri replied, his dark face breaking into a smile. "I haven't seen the catacombs for years. It's time for another visit." Not tall, he was thick-bodied but had no fat on him at all.

"Thanks! I spoke to the boys this morning, reminding them to keep their eyes open and to keep Penny safe. They're very good at that. But I'm happier knowing you'll be along."

The men shook hands and parted. Mr. Daring took a taxi to the Louvre, and Henri sauntered after Penny, Mark, and David.

They took the subway, getting off at the stop for Denfert-Rochereau. There they mounted the subway stairs to the street and walked to the entrance of the catacombs. None of them noticed Henri as he followed them a good way back.

They paid for their tickets, got out their flashlights, and followed a motley assortment of tourists down the narrow, spiral staircase to the tunnel. The guide assembled the group and then led them along a narrow, damp passageway. The cold dampness gripped them at once and they were glad they'd brought their sweaters.

Mark and David maneuvered constantly to keep Penny between them. Yet they did it in such a casual way that she didn't know how carefully they were guarding her. The guide stopped the crowd often to describe the historic places they were passing. Each time he spoke, Penny whispered a translation to David.

David marveled at what she told him. The catacombs had been rock quarries cut by the Romans two thousand years before! Miles and miles of them had been dug in ancient times. Gradually, the city built up over them until the quarries were covered. Then, over the course of centuries, tombs were dug under the growing city; then sewers; then the subway. The city of Paris now sits on literally hundreds of miles of underground passages!

"It's a wonder the whole town doesn't fall in!" Mark observed.

"During the Second World War," Penny whispered to David as they snaked through the narrow passage with the other tourists, "the French Resistance had its headquarters in these underground tunnels. The Germans never found them. They had radios that could reach London and much of France!"

Mark walked ahead of Penny and behind a group of Japanese tourists. David followed behind her. After him came three Frenchmen, burly, powerful men with rough faces, dressed casually in dirty white pants and grey sweaters. They were a solemn group, Penny had noticed, and didn't speak even to each other. Two nice-looking and well-dressed Africans followed the Frenchmen. She hadn't noticed Henri behind the North Africans.

Half the people on the tour had flashlights, it seemed, and their beams threw light in all directions in the narrow tunnel. It gave everyone an eerie feeling.

"Wonder what this was like when people only had torches to light their way?" David asked. "That must have been weird!"

As the guide led them through the narrow passageways, the group strung out behind him in a single file. Mark still walked ahead of Penny, and David was still behind.

Looking back, David was struck by the silent group of Frenchmen who pressed close behind him. They studiously avoided his eyes, but they kept very near. They never spoke to each other, and they didn't seem to look at what the guide was describing. David thought one or two of them seemed familiar but he couldn't remember where or when he might have seen them.

Then the passage widened. They began to enter rooms—rooms filled from floor to ceiling with human bones! Bones stacked neatly, bones arranged casually, bones placed in what might have been humorous designs, but definitely bones—thousands and thousands of bones!

"There are more than three million people buried under Paris!" Penny whispered to David, turning to him in the small crowd that stood before one of the rooms. "Maybe several million more than that!" The lights shone around her face and through her light brown hair as she looked up at him, making it look like spun gold.

Then she turned to listen again to the guide. David

realized that they were jammed in a narrow column of people with no real space to maneuver. He looked over Penny's head, caught Mark's eye, and frowned. Then he nodded his head in the direction of the men behind him.

Mark nodded, but didn't look right away. He waited a minute, listening with the others as the guide explained how the catacombs had become a cemetery for millions of people. Then he glanced casually, briefly, at the men behind David.

Where had he seen those men before? They looked like wrestlers—hardly the type that would be interested in this tour. Mark had the strange sense that he'd seen at least one of them—but where? He didn't like their looks.

The dark walls on either side, the dark ceiling above, the dark floor below, the narrow passage—all began to seem ominous to both David and Mark. They were hemmed in. In fact, Mark thought with alarm, they were trapped!

CHAPTER 15

GRAB THE GIRL!

"**D**avid," Mark said quietly, "swap places for a minute."

David looked puzzled and so did Penny. But he stopped to let Mark squeeze to the rear past Penny; then he moved ahead of her in the passage. Now Mark was between Penny and the three thugs.

The tour began to move again, and David took Penny's hand, urging her to keep up. She realized that the boys sensed danger, and she pressed close to David as he held her hand.

"What's wrong?" she whispered as they crowded along the tight tunnel.

"I don't know," he whispered back, "but we don't like the looks of those men behind us."

His broad shoulders hid the people ahead, so that all she could see were the reflections of other flashlights on the walls and ceiling and her own light on the floor at her feet. She held tightly to David's hand as he led her along the tight passage.

Suddenly she remembered walking with David in the buried temple just a week before, holding his hand, wondering how they were going to get out. She shuddered. Then she began to pray.

Mark had slowed down, deliberately forcing the men following him further back from Penny. But he gave no sign of suspicion as he walked along, looking more carefully now at the walls on either side. He was the typical tourist eager to see all he could.

They had all noticed the old wooden doors they passed periodically—doors to tunnels or basements, the guide said. He'd told them of the miles and miles of interlocking tunnels and how dangerous it was to get off the main path.

"People have wandered away and died, only to be found hundreds of years later," he warned. Penny translated this quickly for David.

They came to a larger room, also filled with bones. Here the tour group stopped together, and the guide gave another brief talk. When he finished, they continued their trek. The passage turned, became narrow again, and curved once more.

Now David and Mark were especially alert. Because of the curving tunnel they could only see a few people ahead or behind them at any one time. David kept his eyes on a large Japanese man who seemed to trail the people ahead. Was this man working with the Frenchmen who were following them?

Then the three saw a small cave to their right, which led to another ancient door, a door of heavy wooden timber with long iron braces. Curiously, it was open!

Penny's grip on David's hand tightened. He glanced

back, worried about Mark's being so close to the men behind. The tunnel was very narrow, the ceiling low. They were boxed in!

Mark's powerful body formed an effective screen between Penny and the men following him. He looked to his right at the cave and the door, keeping the men behind in his side vision. That's how he saw the leading man lunge at him.

Instinctively, Mark pivoted, bringing up his arm in a powerful arc, pinning the man's hand against the stone wall. Then he struck his attacker in the body, knocking the wind out of him, and hit him again as he fell. The thug crumpled to the ground, just as the other men charged. One crashed into Mark; the other brushed past, reaching for Penny.

David whipped around, pushed Penny ahead of him, planted his feet, and struck with great force at the face of the charging man. The Frenchman staggered back, stunned, and clutched his mouth. The other man had knocked Mark into the wall. Mark grunted, then lunged back, his powerful body pivoting at the waist as he punched.

The two North Africans rushed forward—only to be grabbed suddenly from behind by Henri and shoved to the ground.

"Get Penny away, David!" Mark shouted, as he went down, slugging the Frenchman who'd hit him. "Get her away!"

Anguished, David knew he had to do what Mark

said. But the large Japanese man had turned at the noise and stood facing them. David suddenly thought he was hemming them in!

There was only one place to go. Instantly, David pulled Penny with him toward the cave and the opened door. Then he shoved her ahead of him. "Run!" he commanded and turned to help Mark.

Mark was on the ground, struggling with one of the Frenchmen. The first man he'd hit was still down. Henri had disabled one of the Africans and now fought the other. But the third Frenchman rushed toward David to get at Penny.

"Run!" Mark yelled, as he wrestled with the Frenchman.

David kicked suddenly at the charging Frenchman, catching him in the side and knocking him momentarily to his knees. Then David rushed after Penny through the open wooden door. But the tunnel turned sharply, and he saw only blackness ahead.

Suddenly he heard Penny scream! She'd rushed through the door when David released her, around a sharp curve—and into the arms of Hoffmann! The light from her flashlight flooded his face, blinding him for a moment.

The German was as surprised as she was! Instinctively, he clutched her and staggered when she ran into him. But she raised her heavy flashlight and brought it down on his already swollen nose. Yelling with pain, he stumbled back, clutching his bleeding face and blinded now with involuntary tears.

She turned frantically. Then David was beside her!

"Run!" David said, even as he heard the Frenchman coming after him through the door.

Another man suddenly jumped up from a chair behind the reeling Hoffmann!

Penny turned and ran past the temporarily disabled German. David dashed after her, following the beam from her light as it bounced madly ahead. He grabbed his own flashlight from his jeans pocket and switched it on, searching frantically as he ran for something to use as a weapon.

Behind him, the ominous sound of a heavy door slamming shut reverberated through the passage! This was followed by the thud of a bar being thrust into the hinges beside the door. Now no one from the tour could follow to help them. They were on their own, under the giant city, lost in a maze of passageways.

We're trapped! David realized. Sick with apprehension, he ran through the narrow passage with Penny just ahead. Glancing back, he couldn't see his pursuers because of the tunnel's turns. But suddenly he and Penny came to a larger room opening off the passage to their left. It was filled from floor to ceiling with bones!

"Penny! Wait!" he said.

Stuffing his light quickly into his pocket, he reached for a long bone from the pile. As he yanked it loose, the larger Frenchman raced around the corner!

David threw the bone with great force at the man,

then grabbed more, and threw them in rapid succession! The man went down with a yell, and the other man behind him halted for a moment.

Grabbing two of the longer bones, David turned to Penny. "Run! That way!"

Again Penny raced down the narrow passage, the wildly bouncing beam of the light in her hand showing the way through the narrow tunnel. David ran close behind, ready to turn and toss the bones he carried if their pursuers came close. The air was colder here, and both felt chilled in spite of their running.

With a sudden cry, Penny came to a halt. Before them were two doors. The one directly ahead was closed; the other, to the left, was partway open.

"Which way, David?" she asked anxiously. Her face was in deep shadow as the light shone on the wall ahead, but he could hear the fear in her voice. It matched the fear in his heart.

"The open door, Penny! That's got to be the one Hoffmann came through. It must lead us to the ground above."

She dashed through and he followed. Then he had an idea.

"Wait! Shine your light here!" Dropping the bones, he shoved the door closed. This too had a bar standing beside it; David slammed the bar in the two slots. The door was locked!

"Thank the Lord for that! Let's go!" The barred door would keep their pursuers from following for a while at least, he thought. But how long?

They turned and started to run again. Suddenly they heard the men behind them crash into the door they'd locked.

"I don't know how long that'll hold them," David said anxiously. "But it'll help!"

They passed another closed door, this one to their left. Then the tunnel turned sharply right. They ignored another closed door and raced desperately on.

"Where do those lead?" she asked as they ran along in single file.

"I guess to the other tunnels and quarries that honeycomb the city," David answered. "And to stairs that go up to houses. Hoffmann must have come from the ground above, so we're bound to be getting close to where he came in."

Just then they turned a corner and came to a steep stairway directly ahead, visible through a half-opened door. They rushed through the opened door and saw another passage leading away to the left. David turned and closed the door with the bar that fit the slots.

"That should slow them down again!" he said. "Let's rest a minute, Penny! We've got to catch our breath! Then we'll take those stairs. They've got to lead up to the street!"

They paused, breathing deeply, their hearts pounding. Penny looked around. *It's like a coffin*, she thought.

Suddenly they heard heavy feet pounding down the

stairs toward them! "This way, Penny!" David whispered urgently, pointing left to the only way open. He dashed after her, sick at the thought that their way to the street above had been blocked.

CHAPTER 16

THE NET SPREAD WIDE

Back in the tunnel, pandemonium reigned! Frightened people in the tour group were yelling in confusion and alarm. The two Africans and the lone Frenchman lay still and bloodied on the narrow passage floor.

Mark and Henri had tried in vain to open the door through which the Frenchmen had run after Penny and David. It was too strong to break open!

Mark had seen Henri's skill against the men who'd attacked him and trusted him at once. "Follow me, Mark!" the Frenchman said as he rushed back the way they'd come, squeezing past terrified tourists. Mark wondered how the man knew his name and why he was helping him.

"Make way for the police!" Henri said firmly to the people he passed. They shrank against the wall, letting the two men hurry by. Henri and Mark squeezed by almost a dozen people before they broke into a run, heading back to the entrance where the tour had begun.

"We have to go above ground and call for help!"

Henri cried as he ran easily, following the beam of his light along the narrow tunnel. Mark ran behind him, his mind filled with shock and questions about what had happened to Penny and David.

"Thanks for helping out back there! But who are you?" he asked as he ran.

"A friend of your father's," Henri answered. "He thought the danger was past, but he wanted to make sure you three weren't alone in these tunnels. He asked me to keep an eye on you."

"I sure am glad that you did!" Mark said gratefully. "Are you really a policeman?"

"Yes, I'm with the French customs service, and I've been working with your father and Keno. Call me Henri."

They moved quickly. In a few minutes, they reached the spiral staircase and began to ascend. At the top, Mark followed Henri as he ran to the ticket office, identified himself, and asked to use the phone. Mark leaned against the wall to catch his breath as Henri spoke rapidly into the telephone. Mark's French was good, but he wasn't used to the speed with which native Frenchmen talked to each other. It was a struggle for him to keep up with the policeman's short, rapid conversation!

After Henri put down the phone, he thanked the ticket officer and turned to Mark. "Let's go! Vite, Vite!" Quickly the two men went outside. Once on the street, he stopped to explain. "The police will plot the place in the tunnel where we were jumped. They'll be closing in from the other end—and from side entrances as well. I described the stretch of tunnel with the door where your two friends disappeared. They think we can find where that passage ends."

Mark nodded, but his face showed deep distress.

"Don't worry, Mark," Henri said, clapping the sturdy young man on the shoulder. "We'll soon have a net spread wide around these crooks! We'll get your sister and David out very quickly." He looked closely at Mark. "Where did you learn to defend yourself like that? You brought down two strong men!"

"My father taught me. Then he took me to karate instructors for years. He said boys had to learn how to take care of themselves and how to defend others. It's come in handy!" Mark was pleased by the Frenchman's compliment, especially since he was a policeman.

"It came in handy down there today!" Henri agreed, his long face breaking into an appreciative grin.

Then Henri turned to the curb and waved down a cab. Soon they were heading for a nearby police station.

"We have the whole tunnel mapped," he explained, as the cab rushed around a corner. "We know every door and most of the tunnels that connect with them. We think we can find where your sister and David will come out—if they run fast enough to get away from those men."

That was the problem! Would they get away? Two

men had followed them into that door before locking it. Were there others on the other side? With such a maze of passages under the huge city, how would David and Penny know which ones led to the street and safety?

Henri didn't mention his fears to Mark. He didn't have to. Mark knew well enough that the tunnels branched in many directions. Penny and David could turn down any one of scores of passages. Their pursuers could easily trap them in many places under the huge city. They were a long, long way from being safe!

Deep below the street of the great city, Hoffmann leaned against the wall, his handkerchief clutched to his bloodied nose. Everything had gone wrong! A sure plan had collapsed again!

He'd ignored the pounding on the door from the other side. No one from the tour group could force themselves in that way without tools.

But his two men had run off after David and Penny, and he hadn't heard from them since. Weakly, he started to follow them. Then he heard their returning foot steps. They were cursing.

"They locked the door!" one of the men said bitterly. "We couldn't get it open."

Hoffmann knew they'd been beaten. "All those doors have bars. We can't catch them now. Nor can we go back the way we came." He was sick with the taste of defeat.

"But how will we get out?" the other Frenchman demanded. A large man, his face scarred from fights, he was beginning to feel trapped in these underground tunnels. He hadn't wanted to come down here in the first place.

"We'll have to split," Hoffmann said. "You two go back through the door behind you and take the first turn to your left. That takes you to the sewer and from there you can reach the street. I'll go out this door and follow the tour group. They'll never expect that."

He hadn't heard any noise from the other side of the door for some time. Maybe they'd all gone to get the police. He made up his mind. "I'll meet you at the apartment."

Slowly he lifted the bar and placed it against the wall. Then he eased open the door. There was no one there! He closed the door behind him, and then walked rapidly in the direction the tour group had taken.

The tour would be over and the group would be above ground before he got there. He'd emerge unnoticed, then return to the apartment to meet the others.

The two Frenchmen turned and went back into the tunnel. They would take the route to the sewer and go from there to the street.

CHAPTER 17

STALKED IN THE CATACOMBS

Deep beneath the city, David and Penny raced to escape the men running down the steps to head them off. Penny ran in front, following the wildly swinging beam of her flashlight. David followed her, clutching a plank he'd picked up from a pile of loose lumber lying near the door. Behind him, men shouted. Ahead was darkness, lit only by the beam from Penny's light. If they ran into a locked door, they'd be trapped!

The tunnel narrowed, then sloped upward. The ceiling was lower now, and David had to stoop to avoid hitting it. Moisture dripped from the walls to either side; the air was chilled. And they were tired! The passage turned sharply to the right, and a pile of loose stones littered the ground before them.

Penny fell suddenly to her knees, dropping her light. Instantly David was beside her, lifting her to her feet.

"I'm all right," she said, gasping. "I just stumbled on those rocks."

He picked up her flashlight and handed it to her.

"Let's go! They're right behind us."

Then he turned and picked up a couple of large stones. Stepping quickly around the corner of the passage, he hurled them at the approaching men. One glanced off the wall and hit the leading pursuer. The second rock, thrown with all David's might, caught the man in the middle and brought him to a stop, gasping for breath.

The men behind him stopped momentarily, and David took that moment to grab up two more stones before dashing after Penny. Again they ran down the narrow, twisting passage, ducking the low ceiling, avoiding the sharp rocks that protruded from each side of the tunnel.

Suddenly they came to a larger area with passages leading off to the left and to the right. Penny halted, puzzled. David stopped beside her. *Which way should they go?*

The racing footsteps behind them drew nearer.

"That way, Penny!" David said, pointing to his right. She dashed off and he followed, tossing one of his stones through the left-hand passage. The rock bounced and rolled with a terrific noise, as the two of them speeded down the tunnel to the right in their rubber-soled shoes.

Behind them, the three pursuers came to a halt, uncertain which passage to take.

"This way!" the leader shouted, hearing the sound of the rolling rock in the passage to their left. They raced after that sound, following the beams of their lights.

David knew he and Penny would have to stop for breath in a minute. They'd been running a long time! Suddenly they came to another door. This was a massive wooden thing, with long iron bars holding it to the wall. It was partially closed, sagging on its long hinges.

Carefully Penny peeked through the opening, flashing her light. A dingy room with table and chairs met her eyes, and she saw another door in the wall beyond.

"That's all we've got," David said. "Let's take it."

They crossed the room and opened the door.

The narrow passage turned left. They dashed down it for twenty yards or so, and came suddenly upon a pile of stones and debris that rose from the floor and reached two-thirds of the way to the ceiling. They were trapped!

"Oh, David!" Penny said, anguish in her voice.

He stood beside her, sick with apprehension. The men behind might find them any minute. Then he realized that the pile of debris did not reach all the way to the stone ceiling.

"Penny, we've got to crawl up there and hope there's an opening on the other side. There's no place else to go! You go first. I'll stay behind you in case those men come back."

Cupping his hands, he bent and held them for her foot. She grasped his shoulder and stepped into the stirrup formed by his hands. Then she scrambled up

the pile of stones and began to crawl in the narrow
space between them and the walled ceiling. She held
her light in her hand, and saw that the crawl space continued as far as she could see in the narrow passage.

David clambered up the pile of stones with difficulty,
and crawled after her. It was slow going on the rough
stones. *Who piled this stuff here anyway*, he wondered.
*Maybe someone wanted this blocked a long time ago.
Maybe it was blocked ahead.* But they had no place else
to go; those men behind them could return any minute.

Penny attached her light to her shirt and crawled
slowly across the piled rocks. They cut sharply into her
knees and hands. Her back brushed the ceiling some-
times, and she knew that David was cramped more
than she was by the coffin-like passage.

"Oh, David, how long does this go on?" she whispered.

"Let's hope it goes on long enough to get us away
from those men! It's got to end somewhere."

He hated the sensation of being buried! His back
scraped the ceiling each time he moved forward even
though he kept his legs and arms spread out in the low
passage. He'd switched off his light to save power, and
was following Penny's dim form in the light from hers.

Penny thought she'd been crawling an hour! But in
a short while, she noticed that she had more space
between her back and the ceiling. The pile of debris
they were on was sloping gradually downward!

"David, we're going down! I think the rocks are

going down to the ground!" She wanted to shout with joy, but remembered she must whisper.

"You're right!" he replied. He too had more room now, and he crawled more quickly.

"Be careful that you don't fall if the rocks get loose near the bottom," he said quietly.

"Oh, David, I can see the ground now!"

She flashed her light ahead and saw the debris sloping down to the passageway. They were almost on the ground! They scrambled quickly down the slanting pile of stones and reached the tunnel floor.

She turned and threw her arms around his neck. He put his strong arms around her and they stood there rejoicing. "Oh, thank you, Lord," she whispered, her head on his chest. "Thank you, Lord!"

"Amen!" David said fervently.

"Let's move on," he said at last. "We've got to get up to the street somehow." He led the way now, flashlight in hand. She turned hers off to conserve its power. The tunnel widened, and he reached back and took her hand.

"Look!" he said suddenly. His light had flashed upon a steep stairway directly before them!

"Maybe this goes to the street," Penny said hopefully, leaning tiredly against the wall.

"Maybe it does," David agreed. "Let's hope so." They turned and began to climb the steep and narrow stairs.

"Careful, Penny," David warned, as they climbed.

Still he listened for the sound of pursuers behind them, but heard nothing. Maybe that wall of debris had saved them!

Flashing his light before him, he led her upward into the absolute blackness of the narrow tomb-like tunnel. Now they felt terribly constricted again. They came to a landing, a rotted wooden structure with holes in the flooring.

"Let's catch our breath, Penny," he said, leaning against the wall.

"Do you think those men will come after us," she asked quietly, after a moment.

"We'd better plan on it," he replied. "They may run into a blank wall, and then they'll know we came this way. I'm just glad they followed the sound of that rock I threw down the other passage."

"I think we'd better save our batteries," Penny said, switching off her light again.

"Good idea," he agreed, doing the same. Now the darkness engulfed them. He put his arm around her shoulder and held her close. She rested her head against him.

"Oh, David, I hope Mark's all right."

"I think he is," David said. "He knocked down one of those men, and somebody joined him and beat up another. Someone came up from the back to help us and I don't know who he was. But those people on the tour group have had plenty of time to call the police by now. Mark's all right and we will be too! We've just got to keep going until we find the way to the street. Then we'll be safe."

He hugged her close in the darkness. "Ready to go?" he asked.

"I'm ready," she replied.

Switching on his light, he led her up the steep wooden stairs, holding her hand behind him as he climbed. They moved carefully, slowly, not daring to make a false move that would cause them to tumble down. Higher and higher they climbed. The stairs seemed to go on forever.

Suddenly David stopped. There was a door ahead!

"Look!" he whispered.

They stood utterly still in the absolute darkness, hearing nothing but the sound of their own breathing, seeing nothing at all. Leaning against the wall for balance, Penny held tightly to David's hand. They both listened intently.

"I'm going to turn the handle," David whispered. Releasing her hand, he groped for the door, found the handle, gripped it with infinite care and began to turn. Expecting a horrible creak, he was surprised to find that it turned without a sound!

It's been oiled! he thought to himself.

Opening the door slowly, he peered through the crack and into absolute blackness. He opened the door wider, and still there was no light.

"Penny," he whispered, "I'm going to turn on my light for a moment."

He swept the room quickly with the bright beam. It seemed to be a cellar.

"Come on," he said quietly, taking her hand again. Carefully they stepped into the room.

He flashed his light around the room and they saw that it was filled with barrels. A rough wooden table stood in the middle with a bench on each side. Wooden cabinets lined the walls. There were no windows, but there was a door, just opposite the one through which they'd entered.

"Where are we, David?" Penny asked.

"I think it's a cellar. Look at the barrels: probably food and stores and things. Let's head for that door."

"Gosh!" she whispered. "The place is covered with dust and cobwebs. It's probably got a million spiders!"

Quietly, holding her hand, he led her across the floor. Then he turned off his flashlight to check for signs of light from the other side of the door.

There were none. In the utter blackness, he turned to Penny, whose face was just inches from his own. "Penny, if we run into anyone, I'll fend them off while you run for the door and the street. You've got to get to the street for help. That's your job—especially if I'm stopped. O.K.?"

"O.K., David, but I don't want to leave you!" she said anxiously.

"I don't want you to! But if you have to, you can't hesitate. You're our hope of getting help."

"All right," she agreed tremulously.

"Penny, let's ask for the Lord's help." Holding her hand tight, he prayed for their strength and safety. Then he took a deep breath and gripped the door's handle. "Here goes."

Slowly he inched open the heavy wooden door. Flashing the light around, he saw only a very small room! *When will this end?* he wondered.

There were more steep stairs in front of them. But at the top of these, they could see faint signs of light!

Quietly, they crossed the room and came to the stairs. Here they paused.

"Let's go," he whispered, taking her hand again. He led her slowly up the stairs.

They came to another door at the top, around and under which light was seeping. They switched off their flashlights. Carefully he turned the handle and opened the door.

"I see windows!" he whispered excitedly.

Still holding her hand, he led her quietly into the room. Crossing to the far side, they came to a door under which more light was seeping.

He paused and turned to Penny in the almost total darkness. "Penny," he whispered, "we don't know if there's anyone here or not. I'll open this door in a hurry. Remember, if anyone is here, I'll tackle them. You get out to the street."

"O.K., David," she agreed.

He released her hand, held the flashlight to use as a weapon if need be, and quickly opened the door.

CHAPTER 18

THE ESCAPE

The taxi swerved around the corner and slammed to a stop at Henri's command, just behind the parked police sedan.

"Merci, monsieur!" Henri said, handing the driver his fare with a very generous tip. He threw open the door and ran to the sedan; Mark was right behind him.

Two plainclothesmen were leaning against the vehicle, waiting for him. After quick introductions, Henri led the three of them to the door of the building before which the car was parked.

"This is one of the places your sister and David might exit, Mark. Our men haven't seen them yet, however, and they say that no one answers the bell when they ring."

Henri pulled a set of keys from his pocket, selected one, and soon had the door unlocked. Mark followed the three men as they fanned out to cover the room, pistols in their hands.

The curtains were closed. Henri switched on a light and the room brightened. A heavily furnished living room, it was nevertheless empty of people.

"Come with me, Mark," Henri said, moving carefully into the hallway leading to the other rooms on that floor. Henri and Mark then went upstairs, while the other men searched below. But they found no one.

"The cellar door is jammed shut, Henri," one of the men told him when they returned to the hallway. "No one could have used it."

"Let's go!" Henri commanded instantly, leading the way outside.

With a sinking heart Mark began to wonder how long this would take. What was happening to Penny and David? Had they been captured by the men who set that trap underground? If they had, the men could have taken them almost anywhere under the city by this time!

Not far away, David eased open the door of the dark kitchen and looked into a dining room. He saw a long table surrounded by high-backed chairs on each side, a china cabinet, and two long shuttered windows in the far wall. There was no one in the room, and no sound came from the room that opened off to his left.

Penny followed close behind as David moved quietly into the dining room, between the long table and the wall. They made no sound on the thickly carpeted floor.

They came to the door. Here David paused and looked carefully into the hall. Penny stood quietly behind him, her flashlight held ready as a weapon if need be.

Daylight seeped into the dining room through cracks in the shutters, and into the hall from two clear panes of glass that bordered the thick wooden door to the street. Penny was struck by the musty smell of the long-closed room.

David looked across the hall to the front door, searching for the lock. He wanted to find it before they got there. There it was—with a long iron key protruding from it.

Turning to Penny, he pointed to the lock, and whispered, "Cross the hall to that door, turn the lock, then run into the street!"

She nodded, trembling.

She went straight for the door, while he turned to his left, facing the entrance of the large room that opened up before him.

He took his stance in the hall directly behind her, as she moved to the door and turned the key.

The handle moved easily, without a sound. Penny turned it completely, then pushed the door open. Glancing gratefully toward David, she stepped through the door and ran down the steps to the street.

David followed her and closed the door carefully behind him. Then he ran down the steps to join Penny. They were free! They'd reached the street!

Their hearts were pounding as they fled the building. They were free! David looked left and then right, scanning the street.

"Now we've got to find a cab or a phone!" he said jubilantly.

"This way!" he called, taking Penny's hand and turning to the right. Hand in hand they raced along the sidewalk. passing the tall buildings constructed so long ago, searching anxiously for a taxi.

There was a yell behind them! David whipped his head around and saw three men emerge from a nearby house and start running after them!

"Someone's recognized us!" he said, heart sinking.

"Oh, David!" she exclaimed as they ran, holding tightly to his hand. "I thought we'd *never* get out of all those tunnels! Now they're chasing us again."

"Look for a cab!" he said, as they ran toward the intersection.

Glancing back as they rounded the corner, David saw the men still racing after them.

"Hurry, Penny!" he said, as they increased their pace. People stared as they ran past, weaving among tourists and townspeople in their mad dash for safety. A narrow lane opened to their right, and David turned instinctively into it, pulling Penny with him. There were no people in this alley between the tall dark buildings, and they ran freely, swiftly, their fitness and practice standing them in good stead.

But behind them the three men ran swiftly also. They too came to the corner and turned it. They spied the youngsters dart into the narrow passage and rushed after them, scattering people in their charge.

David saw an even smaller lane open to the left and turned into it, pulling Penny with him. The two ran twenty-five paces or so in this very narrow passage, wondering where it would end. Suddenly it made a turn and stopped before a wall! It was six or seven feet high.

"Quick, Penny!" David said, cupping his hands together once again to form a stirrup for her feet. "Climb up the wall and I'll follow you."

She placed her foot in his clasped hands, put her hands on his shoulders, stepped up, and reached her arms for the top of the wall. He pushed her upward and she crawled over the top, held on for a moment, then dropped to the ground below. David leaped up, grabbed the top of the wall, and pulled his body up just as he heard his pursuers yell behind him.

Dropping to the ground, he told Penny to run.

David glanced down and saw loose stones larger than his fist strewn around a pile of planks. Grabbing two of the stones he tossed them into the air and over the wall. Stooping to grab more, he threw these also in a continuing stream. The stones crashed on the street beyond the wall, and some hit the men below! David heard them yell as they were struck.

He whirled around and dashed after Penny. She'd reached the end of the narrow alley. Gasping for breath, she was waiting for him on the street.

"This way!" he said, running into the broader avenue, looking left and right. Still no cab was in sight!

The street was crowded, and David and Penny had to move more slowly. David looked back repeatedly to see if their pursuers were in sight, but he saw no trace of them yet. But they might appear at any moment, and he knew he and Penny couldn't afford to stop their flight.

They passed a couple of outdoor cafes. People sat in the chairs eating and drinking, reading books and newspapers, talking and smoking. Turning a corner, they saw several more cafes, and these too were half-filled with customers.

"Let's go into this one!" David said suddenly, pulling Penny inside a larger cafe. Instantly, they were in darkness and their eyes had to adjust to the change in light. David searched for a booth, saw a vacant one in the back along the right wall and led Penny to it. Swiftly they slipped into the seat, facing the street. Penny sat next to the wall; David was beside her. By sliding to his left he could put himself out of sight from anyone entering the front door.

For the first time in a long time, they breathed a sigh of relief. The waiter came, a tall man in a dark suit with a white apron, and Penny ordered Perrier for them both. Then the two sank back, exhausted, in the seat. He put his arm around her; she rested her head on his shoulder.

"I'll call your dad from that phone over there," he said a few moments later. "He'll call the police. In the meantime, no one can take us out of this cafe. In fact, they won't even find us. There are too many places for three men to search."

The waiter brought their Perriers. Neither moved for a few minutes. Then he looked into her eyes. "You've got to be thirsty after all the running we've done!" He smiled.

She smiled back. "I guess I am."

CHAPTER 19

ON TO CARCASSONE!

That evening, Mark, Penny, and David, Mr. and Mrs. Daring, Keno, and Henri were eating at a small restaurant, Mrs. Daring's favorite. They'd discussed the strange events of the past two days, and marveled at the persistence of Hoffmann's people in pursuing the wealth of the ancient Egyptian treasures.

"They had a great plan!" Mr. Daring conceded as the waiter brought their food. "But, once again, you three spoiled their plans!" He looked with undisguised pride at each of them in turn.

"Dad, you said a minute ago that something happened in the street yesterday to wreck their first attack. What was it?" Mark asked.

Henri answered before Daring could speak. "It was two Russian Wolfhounds, a tomato cart, and a nun." He laughed.

The kids were astonished. "You mean those big dogs we saw coming from the market?" Penny asked incredulously. She wore the lovely white dress that David liked so much, and he thought she looked beautiful.

"That's right, Penny," Henri replied. "Those dogs stopped a well-planned attempt to steal your camera case with the pictures Keno had taken of the Egyptian tablet. They were going to take you too if necessary."

"How did the dogs stop them?" David asked. He and Mark and the other men had dressed in coats and ties to come to the elegant restaurant. "We only saw them walk by."

Henri explained, laughing. "We got the whole story from the men we took to the police station. They were happy to tell everything. They know they're in very big trouble!"

He laughed again as he continued. "The Turks threw Hoffmann's big man into the river. Then they threw Hoffmann in as well! Most of them are in jail now."

The kids tried to take all this in, but it was too improbable.

"With all due respect to the French police, Henri," Daring said, "that story's hard to believe. Wolfhounds and tomato carts, and nuns stopping Hoffmann and his professional thugs!"

"It is indeed, Jim. I hardly believe it myself," Henri laughed. "But it's what the police have put together from questioning those men."

"In other words," Daring said, "half of Hoffmann's team was taken out of the fight before they could go for the kids!"

"That's right."

"But what about Hoffmann himself?" Penny asked. "Have you captured him yet?"

"Not yet, Penny," Henri admitted. "But we got the men in the tunnel with him—the ones chasing you. And we got the men Mark and I fought. But I'm sorry to say Hoffmann himself got away."

"Once again," Daring said quietly with a frown.

The kids were quiet, thoughtful. Hoffmann always got away. And he always came back. When would they see him again?

"That was great fighting you two did in the catacombs," David said quietly. His face was troubled. "I sure hated to run off and leave you."

"You did the right thing, David," Jim Daring said, leaning forward and looking seriously into the young man's eyes. "That's the only reason Penny's with us tonight. Carolyn and I can never thank you enough."

"Well, I wouldn't have left Penny, of course," he said, "but it was hard to run away and leave Mark and Henri to face the fight."

"I know it was," Mr. Daring replied. "But you each did your duty, and the Lord protected you all."

"Well, this is too much!" Carolyn Daring said firmly. "These poor kids have faced danger from crocodiles on the river back in Africa, then danger from Hoffmann's men in that underground Egyptian tomb. And now they've been chased in Paris, of all places. Whoever heard of such things!" She looked indignant. "They don't seem to be safe anywhere!"

Her husband started to protest, but she continued.

"I know, and I'm not saying it's your fault, Jim. But I insist that it's time for them to have a real vacation, where they'll be safe. Let's take them to Carcassonne tomorrow."

"You are absolutely right, Carolyn," her husband agreed. "Nothing's worked out as we'd thought it would. We'll all go to Carcassonne."

The next morning, Mark, David, and Penny were enjoying a last pastry at their favorite outdoor restaurant on the Place Maubert. Another beautiful blue sky shone above them while the bustling pedestrian life of this great international city surged past.

"Tell me again what you call these things," David said as he savored the treat the waiter had brought.

"It's called *madeleines*," Penny replied, "and the French love them."

"I'm not sure we need to leave Paris so soon," Mark said thoughtfully, finishing another bit of his rich chocolate pastry. "After all, there's so much culture we haven't taken in yet. What do you think, David?"

"You've got a point, Mark. How can we leave this city of museums and history and music, just for a jaunt to an old medieval fortress?"

"It's not just an 'old medieval fortress'," Penny objected. "It's the finest surviving walled city in Europe. It's got two ancient walls surrounding really historic houses and churches. There's nothing like it left—they've all been destroyed." Ever ready for new adventures, she had her camera case hung on the back of her chair and had already bought plenty of film.

"I don't know," Mark said. "It's a shame to rush through life without soaking up culture. And Paris has a lot of culture for us to soak up."

"And Carcassonne has a lot of chocolate you can soak up too!" Penny replied with a laugh. "Which seems to be all you Philistines really care about anyway."

David's lean face took on a hurt expression. Leaning back in the chair beside Penny, he came to the defense of his friend. "Listen to her, Mark!" he said. "If we didn't eat to keep up our strength, we'd be too weak to protect her. How would we fight off the Hoffmanns of this world?"

"That's the truth!" Mark agreed. "In fact, we're the ones who make civilization possible. Who'd be able to take the time to make these pastries if there weren't people strong enough to fight off the bad guys?"

"May I join you," a voice behind them asked. None of them had seen Sandra come up.

"Sure," Mark replied. Penny gave the sad girl a welcoming smile as the two boys got up. Mark pulled out the chair beside him, and Sandra smiled her thanks and sat down.

"Did you meet Mom this morning?" Penny asked.

"Oh, I did! Thanks for asking her to talk with me! She helped so much. She's found a home for me to stay in for the next month, or more if I want to. A

French family who keep a pension—sort of a bed and breakfast. And they speak English. I can help with the shopping and housecleaning. And they've got a friend who can help me with my painting!" Sandra seemed genuinely please.

"Want us to wander off so you girls can talk?" Mark asked.

"Oh, no," Sandra answered. She looked at Penny. "I did want you to know that I told Steve we're through, and I feel so much better!"

"Did he call you? I thought he'd disappeared," Penny replied, showing her surprise.

"Oh, he always calls after he walks off. He gives me another chance to give in and do what he wants. This time I said we're through. He didn't believe me at first." Her light blue eyes showed her determination. "I told him I was through with him and with that kind of life." She paused, her face red. "He told me I was crazy."

"How did you answer that?" Penny asked quietly. Mark and David kept very still, not wanting to interrupt. Clearly, the girl had made a major decision.

"I told him that 'crazy' was what I had been—but not anymore! He said some nasty things then. But I didn't argue, Penny. I just told him that I'd decided to choose a different kind of life. That I'd learned there were some good men in this world, and that I wasn't going to waste my life with guys who lived only for themselves."

She thought a moment. "I can't blame him, of

course. He was the kind of guy I thought I wanted, and I was the kind of girl he was looking for. We suited each other. Actually, we both used each other." Her face was sad; yet she showed real resolve.

Mark wanted to say how much they respected her, but he didn't know how. "Still no word from your parents?" he asked.

"No. Dad's gone to Mexico with his new wife, and Mom's gone on a business trip." She rose. "Well, I just wanted to say hi, and tell you thanks for letting me meet your Mom. She's going to see me next week when you get back from Carcassonne."

"We'll see you too," Penny said warmly. "Take care!"

Smiling faintly, Sandra walked off.

"She's made a big decision, hasn't she?" Mark observed. "That wasn't easy."

Penny nodded. "Mom told me last night that when she talked with Sandra, she didn't press the gospel on her because she didn't seem to be ready. So Mom just tried to show from experience where Sandra's present way of life would lead her—and the inevitable misery it brings. And Mom told her that there were really good men around, like you two!"

"Well, I hope she didn't stretch things too far," Mark said.

"How could she?" Penny replied, smiling. "You boys are wonderful. I think Mom really succeeded in telling her there were better options than the ones she'd been choosing. The family that agreed to take her in is Christian. They've done this for other kids and they'll make her feel at home."

"I admire her," David said. "It takes courage to make a change like that."

Behind Penny sat a middle-aged woman in a tight red dress. She pushed her dark glasses higher on her nose as a man approached her table from the street. Instantly, she dropped her fork, which clattered to the pavement.

"Oh!" she exclaimed, as she turned and leaned over to pick it up. Retrieving the fork, she straightened and quickly slipped an envelope into the side pocket of Penny's camera case, which hung on the back of her chair. Neither Penny nor the boys noticed what the woman had done; nor did the man who was approaching the woman's table.

Tall, sharply dressed in a dark pin-striped suit, he walked to her table, greeted her without smiling, and pulled out a chair across from her.

"You did not bring the letter to my office," he said quietly in French.

"You did not release my son, as you had promised," she replied evenly. Her knuckles were white as she closed her hands and placed them in her lap.

"There was a problem," he said.

"Solve it, if you wish to see that letter," she answered.

"We will," he said emphatically, "so give it to me at once." He leaned forward with a hard look. "You know we will not allow those names to fall into the hands of the police."

"Then give me my son and you'll get the letter." She took off her glasses. He could see that she had been crying. But, obviously, she wanted him to know that she was deadly serious.

"Listen," she said firmly. "You won't find that letter on me. You'll never find it unless you release my son, at once!"

For a long moment he stared at her without speaking. He believed her. Sighing, he took a small radio from his pocket and spoke quietly into it. "Bring him at once!"

"He is coming," he said to the woman as he returned the radio to his coat pocket. They waited without speaking.

Several minutes later, a young man rounded the corner and hurried toward the table. A scowling and powerfully built man followed him very closely.

With a glad cry, the woman rose and rushed to greet her son.

The man at the table jumped up from his chair and hurried after her. "The letter!" he hissed. "Give me the letter!"

Turning, she came to her senses. They were delivering her son; she would deliver the letter. "There," she pointed. "In that girl's camera case!"

But it wasn't there! The camera case into which she had stuffed the letter was no longer hanging from the back of Penny's chair—it was gone!

Frantically, she looked around her. Penny and the two boys were at the street, entering a taxi. "There it is! On that girl getting into the cab!"

Mark gave the driver the address of their hotel, and the taxi pulled out from the curb. Desperately, the two men dashed to the street and flagged another cab.

None of the Americans noticed the cab that began to follow them.

"I'm going to miss that cafe," Mark said.

"So will I," David agreed.

"Me too!" Penny added. She was squeezed between the two boys with David's arm around her, and she was happily contemplating the wonderful city they were about to visit. "But Dad said to be back at the hotel by noon. I'm already packed."

"And to think, we'll be riding on the fast train!" she continued, her eyes shining with pleasure as she looked up at David.

"At two hundred miles an hour!" David marveled. "That's fast!"

"It sure is!" Mark agreed emphatically. He glanced pointedly at David's arm around Penny's shoulder. "We'll both have to hold on to you, Penny, to make sure you don't fall off!" He grinned broadly at the two of them.

"Ouch!" he exclaimed suddenly, as Penny stamped on his foot.

The taxi raced through the busy streets of Paris, taking them back to their hotel where they'd collect their suitcases and join Mr. and Mrs. Daring for a trip on the fastest train in Europe.

They were on their way to the fabled city of Carcassonne!